THE DUST-COVERED
DAYS OF *Dorie Archer*

THE DUST-COVERED DAYS OF *Dorie Archer*

Barbara Eymann Mohrman

BARBARA EYMANN MOHRMAN

ILLUSTRATIONS BY WAVA J. BEST

BERN STREET
PUBLISHING

OMAHA, NEBRASKA

ISBN: 978-0-9884174-4-1
LCCN: 2013935523

The recipes included in this book should not be tried without adult supervision. The homemade remedy for cough should never be tried. It is included here to show what people did in the 1930s without modern medicine.

The illustrator, Wava J. Best, used vintage photos from the Eymann Family Private Collection and her imagination as models for her drawings of Dorie Archer and her family life.

Printed in the United States of America
10 9 8 7 6 5 4 3 2 1

To my cousins.
-Barbara Eymann Mohrman

In loving memory of my parents who where born in 1909 and 1910. They had the same struggles and rewards as the Archer family while living in Nebraska during the 30s.

To my loving husband Tom and our family; Jody, Thomas; Pam, Marty, Sean, and Kyle; Vikki, Lance, Jack, and Drew.
–Wava J. Best

A multidisciplinary curriculum guide is available for The Dust Covered Days of Dorie Archer. Primary source video interviews of the Eymann family are available. To obtain these please contact Barbara Eymann Mohrman at Barbara@BernStreet.com.

Contents

Introduction 1

Characters 5

Prologue 6

1   The Archers of Nebraska 9

2   A Sled and a Risky Rescue 17

3   The Boys of Summer 26

4   Dust, Darkness, and Danger 32

5   Monsters of Mayhem 41

6   The Chokecherry Secret 55

    Recipe for Chokecherry Jelly 62

7   Duster! 63

8   Runners and Clean Up 69

9   Fight Back, Maggie! 79

10   The Best Choice 83

11   The Wonder of Bread 90

12   The Shoe That Did Not Cooperate 94

    Recipe for Corn Meal Mush 105

    Recipe for Homemade Soap 106

13   I Double Dog Dare You! 108

14   Saturday Night in the City 115

Acknowledgments 127

About the Author and Illustrator 129

Introduction

I WROTE THIS BOOK AFTER speaking to students about the dust bowl years of the 1930s in Nebraska. I found that while many of them had read about the dust bowl in a textbook, few of the students understood the daily struggles of life during this era and just how dangerous and difficult life was for the people of Nebraska.

I was fortunate to have family members who lived through this time. I interviewed them and researched their stories. I listened intently as a television crew recorded their stories. At that moment I decided to write a book that would be entertaining for students and a learning experience too. The experiences of my parents and my aunts and uncles were too valuable to be lost to time.

The stories and events in this book are true. I combined the experiences of my family, the Eymanns of Oakdale, Nebraska, as well as the experiences of my aunts and uncles who married into the Eymann family into one book. I created the Archer family, but everything that happens to them actually happened in real life.

Braving the duster!

The term *dust bowl* is often used to describe the period in American history of severe dust storms that roared across the nation during the 1930s. These storms caused major ecological and agricultural damage to the prairies of America especially from 1934 to 1938. These storms were called dusters, black blizzards, and black rollers.

The dust bowl began in Texas and Oklahoma. Wheat was planted year after year. Even the native grasses were plowed up and planted into wheat. This continual planting exhausted the topsoil. In 1931 there was a bumper crop of wheat. The supply of wheat far outweighed the demand. The price of wheat fell and farmers went broke. Many of them gave up and migrated to California in search of a better life. During the years 1930 to 1931 a period of severe drought began. With no rain and intense heat, the depleted soil—abandoned with no crops planted—dried up and turned to dust. Without the natural anchor of native grass to hold it down, this soil blew away with the wind.

The drought reached record proportions in 1934 to 1936, and the years of dust storms began. The clouds of dust reached far up into the sky as the dusters rolled over much of the mid-section of the country, blocking out the sun and suffocating the people and animals who lived there.

Nebraska was not spared. The dust piled up in the ditches of Nebraska and covered the fields and farms. The devastation continued with the arrival of swarms of grasshoppers. These hungry hoppers ate the sparsely growing crops down to the dirt. They returned year after year to wreak havoc on the farms of Nebraska.

This is the story of the people who stayed to farm their land. They fought the grasshoppers, the drought, and the dusters. These people persevered in the face of incredible adversity. They problem-solved, made do with what was on hand, and never gave up. They learned the hard lesson of what can happen when people do not take care of the land. This is a story of the spirit of Nebraska.

It is my hope that students will learn about this era in our history through the Archer family and realize that the people who lived in the 1930s through dusters and swarms of grasshoppers had hobbies, hopes, and dreams, just like today's students do. I hope students will realize that the futures of these people were changed and affected by the devastating results of the dust bowl. My hope is for understanding and learning.

Characters

Stanley Archer, Father
Anna Archer, Mother

Children:
Michael, nicknamed Mick, sixteen years old
Marlene, nicknamed Marley, fourteen years old
Doris, nicknamed Dorie, eight years old
Robert, nicknamed Robbie, five years old
Margaret, nicknamed Maggie, the baby, one year old

This story takes place from 1934 to 1938 in Oakdale, Nebraska.

Prologue

THE FURIOUS FLUTTERING OF BIRDS flying low was the first sign that something was wrong. The squawks and shrieks of the disturbed birds echoed through the farm yard. The chorus of their frightened cries scared eight-year-old Dorie Archer.

Suddenly Dorie felt cold. She wrapped her arms around her body to keep warm as she looked at the anxious faces of her brothers and sister. She was sure the temperature had dropped at least twenty degrees in the past few minutes.

Her eyes inspected the darkening sky. An ominous black cloud hung low over the horizon in the softly rolling hills of this rural farming community. Its volume seemed to rise for miles into the sky or at least it appeared that way to Dorie. She had never seen any storm like the one approaching the farm now. Was this perhaps a spring thunderstorm or, worse yet, a tornado? Batches of birds flew frantically past her as they attempted to wing their way to safety and out of the destructive path of the quickly advancing cloud.

Suddenly, the black cloud of dust descended, enveloping everything within it. Dorie had never seen anything as inky black as that cloud. She watched as a bunch of birds was caught up in the revolving dust and debris and disappeared into the shadowy depths of the cloud.

Dorie Archer only knew she had to get out of that black gale before it suffocated her. She rapidly gulped in small doses of air in an attempt to breathe only to be rewarded with a mouthful of choking dust. The air was churning now as tumbleweeds flew by the Archer children. The cloud that only minutes before had been in the distance was upon them.

The wind began to swirl around them and pick up in intensity. The cloud cast a veil over them as thick as pea soup. Soon the sun was completely blotted out by its murkiness. The light had turned into total darkness that Sunday afternoon.

Imprisoned within the swirling, blinding wind, the children could feel particles of dust blast their faces sharply as they frantically covered their mouths and eyes with their arms and hands. It was no use. The dust filled their mouths with grit and stung their eyes. It coated their teeth and tongue and caused them to cough, sputter, and struggle for air.

Dorie bent her head into the withering gale of wind that assaulted her and covered her mouth with both hands. She fought hard to maintain her balance and move toward the house. Above the roaring din she could hear her parents, Anna and Stanley, calling out their names, "Mick, Marley, Dorie, Robbie."

But she could not answer for fear of ingesting an even more massive amount of dust. Dorie started to cry. Dirty tears rolled down her cheeks as she fought with all of her might against the wind and the dust.

What is this? she wondered. *What makes this wind and dust roar through our farm? How and when will it ever stop?* She had no answers for those questions as she willed her feet to keep moving forward through the sooty, filthy curtain of fierce wind. Dorie felt powerless, frightened, and alone against the might of this great force of nature as she and her brothers and sister made their way to the farm house and shelter from the worst dust storm ever to hit Nebraska.

The Archers of Nebraska

ONE SEASON WAS FALLING AWAY and another beginning. The Nebraska wind carried the smell of dry leaves through the autumn air. The late afternoon sun burned a reddish orange that gave everything a dull glow. Doris Archer, always known as Dorie, trudged dutifully up the dirt road that led from the highway to the farm house she called home.

Her black school shoes were already covered with a film of parched soil that seemed to be everywhere in Oakdale, Nebraska, this fall. Each footstep Dorie took raised puffs of the dried, barren, and parched earth into the air as she walked toward her farm house. The school day was over. Dorie was suspended for a few moments in that in-between state of school time and home time. These few minutes provided her with time to think over her day.

Dorie loved her one-room school house, and she especially loved her teacher, Miss Hayes. Dorie loved the smell of chalk and the efficient way Miss Hayes wrote in her carefully scripted handwriting on the blackboard. She loved the way the pages of her *Reader* felt as she leafed through the smooth, well-worn sheets of paper. She breathed in the musty odor of that paper as her brown eyes eagerly took in the words of the story.

Sometimes her mind wandered as eight-year-old Dorie listened to Miss Hayes giving lessons to both the younger and the older children in the red-brick country school. Dorie's chestnut hair was cut into a straight bob by her father in the family kitchen. Her thick tresses hung to her firm chin. Her bangs were held back away from her oval face with a black bow.

Dorie's brown eyes were intelligent and serious but often danced with humor as she shared jokes with those around her. Her long straight nose led to a mouth that was a bit off center but always slightly turned up into a hint of a smile. Dorie was good natured and kind.

Her sturdy frame was covered by her favorite dress sewn by her mother and covered with red hearts and crimson flowers. Dorie always wore her shiny black shoes to school. She believed it when her mother said, "Dress your best to do your best." Her skin glowed brown as a berry from the hours in the summer sun.

Dorie was a happy girl and was content to do her school work and to learn as much as she could. Dorie felt safe within the confines of the solidly built structure and the guidance of Miss Hayes.

As she approached the farm her eyes scanned the fields of yellowing corn stalks. For the last few years the summers in Nebraska had become blistering hot. It seemed to Dorie that less rain fell each passing summer. The ground that grew the crops they lived on became drier and dustier. This fall her father was harvesting the corn but with scant rain this past few months Dorie knew the corn harvest would be meager.

Dorie could see her father, Stanley, out in the fields, working to pick the dried out ears of corn. Their team of horses, Molly and Dan, was hitched to the wagon where her father tossed the corn he picked by hand. Without aiming, Stanley would toss the corn toward the bang board of the wagon letting the corn hit it and fall solidly into the bottom of the wagon. It was hard work!

Dorie watched as Molly enthusiastically pulled the wagon to keep pace with Stanley's work. Dorie laughed as she saw that Dan lagged a bit behind, content to allow Molly to do most of the work. Dorie giggled again at the sight and a smile lingered on her lips as she thought about how much she loved them both—faults and all.

Molly and Dan were essential to her father and the farm work, but they also provided the family with their only form of transportation. Dorie's father would hitch the horses to the wagon to take the Archer family into town to church or to Taylor's grocery store. Dorie sighed as she thought about those rides because most of her transportation was provided by her own two feet.

Dorie glanced over her shoulder to see if her brother Michael and her sister Marlene were close. Michael was nicknamed Mick and he was near sixteen years old now, and from what Dorie observed at school and church he was very popular with the girls. They were always hanging around him and oohhing and aahhing over his every word.

Mick was not tall but he was very strong. His muscles came from all the farm work he did to help his father. His skin was caramel colored from the hours working in the hot sun and his eyes were a smoky brown color. He was quiet and at times it was difficult to decide what he was thinking. But his eyes twinkled merrily if there was an adventure to be had.

Dorie guessed the girls thought Mick was handsome, but she laughed to think if only those girls could see him chasing around Mom's chickens or crammed into the tiny tin bath tub in the family kitchen. Dorie decided maybe then they wouldn't think he was so handsome.

At fourteen years of age, Marlene, nicknamed Marley, was a thin, upright girl who took life seriously. Her long auburn hair was braided and hung down her back. Her face was an open book with the same brown eyes as her brother. Those eyes seemed to take in everything around her. She, too, was quiet but was not the risk taker her brother was. In fact, the opposite was true.

Marley was the cautious Archer, always taking care and watching out for others. She was her mother's right hand, assisting her with everything from sewing to gardening to canning to caring for her siblings. She was a determined girl and most always kind to Dorie if at times just a little too bossy. Sometimes Dorie felt as if she had two mothers instead of one.

They carried their school books fastened by a strap and slung over their shoulders. Marley called out, "Dorie, your books are tilted a bit. Tighten them up now and be careful as they might slip out. Then what would mother say?"

Dorie scrunched her face into a mischievous smile and glared back at Marley. She knew Marley was trying to be helpful but gosh oh golly sometimes she just wished her big sister would leave her alone and let her fend for herself.

Each night the Archer children did their homework together by the light of the kerosene lamp. Of course, this was after they did their chores of milking the cow, cleaning out the barn or chicken coop, feeding the chickens, gathering wood for the stove and either helping their mother clean, cook, and care for the two younger children and do dishes or help their father in the fields. There was always something to do around the farm and everyone had to pitch in and help.

Stanley and Anna Archer, Dorie's parents, did not own the farm they lived on. Stanley was the hired man for George Hunter who owned many acres of farmland and several farm houses. Stanley was the perfect man for the job. He was tall and lanky. He was hard working and honest.

Stanley Archer did all of Mr. Hunter's farm work. It was a big job but in return Mr. Hunter rented the farm house, barn, and a plot of land to the Archer family. The Archers could keep a cow, some chickens, and grow corn, beans, potatoes, and tomatoes on the plot of land in order to feed their family. Anna canned these delicious, fresh vegetables in the fall, and with the eggs and meat from the chickens, and milk, cream, and butter they made themselves from their cow, the family got by.

Worry creased Dorie's brow as she continued her walk home. Each passing year the harvest got smaller and smaller. There just was not enough rain to make the crops grow and the blazing sun

Anna and Maggie.

withered the plants in the fields. The heat and the drought were drying up the good Nebraska crops and land.

At night after her parents put the kids to bed and her siblings were asleep, Dorie would listen to her parents' hushed voices. From these discussions Dorie knew they were worried about how to feed their family through the winter, but Dorie also knew her parents would find the answer. She then fell asleep each night secure in their love and protection for the future.

Dorie climbed up the worn wooden steps of the porch leading into her farm house. She flung the door open and dropped her school books onto an oak bench.

She called out to her mom as she did every day, "Mother, home again! What chore should I do first?"

Anna appeared in the doorway leading to the kitchen. Anna was quite small, almost doll-like in stature. Her brown hair was pulled back from her face and held in place by a clasp although curly tendrils framed her round, cheerful face. She was always smiling, especially if her children were nearby.

Anna wore her everyday dress of printed yellow flowers, but it could barely be seen underneath the apron she wore. Anna did not have many clothes, but she had an abundance of aprons all hand sewn from scraps of old clothing. She wore one every day to keep her dress clean as she worked around the house and farm yard. She kept her Sunday-go-to-meeting dress in the closet.

She used the apron as a tea towel, table wiper, dust rag, and kid nose wiper. She held up the ruffled edges and formed the apron into a cloth basket. In the cloth basket she placed the chicken feed and with her hands she would spread it out on the yard for

Anna's apron.

the clucking, hungry chickens to feed on. Anna always had a tea towel slung over her shoulder. Dorie could not remember a time when it was not there.

"Heavenly days, girl, where are your brother and sister? Come here and give me a hug and a kiss. I have sorely missed you all today. Your little brother is so anxious to have you read them a story. Maggie is still napping but Robbie is out back playing with the wagon. Go on now and tell him you are home but grab an apple for a snack first. You can go out to the milk cellar and fetch the bucket. It is fresh milk from this morning. Your brother and sister may be thirsty too after a long day at school," Anna directed her daughter.

Dorie did not have to be told twice. She grinned. Her younger siblings were a captive audience, and she loved playing "teacher" with them almost as much as she loved her day at school. But most of all Dorie loved her mother's welcoming smile and the warmth of her family in their Nebraska farm home.

Wooden milk bucket.

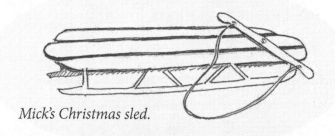

Mick's Christmas sled.

A Sled and a Risky Rescue

WINTER 1935

"IT'S MY TURN NOW," FIVE-YEAR-OLD Robbie yelled to his big brother Mick from the top of the river bank.

"You just hold your horses," Mick shouted back to him, "this was my Christmas present, remember? I am going to give it the first test run and then all of you will get your turn."

The Archer children had celebrated a subdued Christmas this year. The paltry harvest from this last fall had not provided the family with enough food to can for the winter, not to mention the luxury of surplus money for buying Christmas presents. Anna and Stanley had scrambled to find some gifts for the children and had managed to scrape a few things together with the help of their relatives.

Mick's sled was actually a hand-me-down from an older cousin. It had been used but was in fine shape. Marley had received a winter coat. It had also belonged to her older cousin, but Anna's nimble fingers had remade the coat into one that looked brand new. Dorie had received hair ribbons that Anna had created out of scraps of material. Dorie was pleased because the ribbons matched her handed-down dresses now.

Robbie's gift was an old red wagon, also donated from an older cousin. Stanley had repainted the worn spots, removed the rust from the wheels as best he could, and painted the handle a rich black color. Robbie had already used the wagon to haul the dog and cats around the farm yard.

Maggie was too little to care what she got, but Anna had made a cornhusk doll for her. She had sewn clothes for the doll from the twenty-pound flour sacks they bought at Taylor's grocery store. Nothing was wasted and the children were content with their treasures.

Dorie's cheeks were pink with excitement and the cold as the children pulled the sled up to the steep bank of the river for a test. The snowstorms of winter had subsided but had left inches of the white, powdery substance on the ground. The biting cold that had gripped Nebraska that December had eased a bit. The conditions were just right for the trial run of the sled. The steep incline of the river bank was the perfect location because the sled could swoosh down the snowy hill and careen out onto the ice-covered river. The river bank on the other side was a natural backstop for the speeding sled.

The bright sun shone warmly on Dorie's face as she followed Marley and Mick to the hill. It felt good to be outside, and it felt particularly good to have the sunshine. It had been days since they had seen so much sun. She and Marley were both wearing their warmest gray woolen socks pulled up to their thighs. Their winter coats were buttoned tightly and mittens covered their cold hands. Both girls wore woolen scarves tied beneath their chins, and well-worn boots covered their feet.

Dorie wondered, *Why is it that the boys never felt the cold as much as girls?* She watched Mick and Robbie pulling the sled with their coats loosely gathered around them, mittens and scarves thrown aside. The boys' only other protection from the cold was a cap each one kept pulled down over their ears.

"Wait a minute before you go, Robbie," Mick said, "I want to sharpen the runners a bit more." Robbie could barely contain his excitement because he knew the sled would accelerate even faster with sharp runners and he was eager to try it. He watched as Mick swiped the blade of the scythe over the runners of the sled.

"Marley, you're next!" Robbie called to her from over his shoulder as the sled flew down the hill toward the frosty river. Robbie laughed out loud as the sled hit the ice and skidded toward the opposite bank where it would stop in the bushes.

As Robbie pulled the sled back up the hill, Marley arranged her outdoor clothing neatly. "Now, Mick, no more sharpening the runners. I don't want the sled to be out of control. I just want a nice, safe ride," Marley begged Mick.

But he was already at work on the steely runners. Marley got on and held tightly as they gave her a push. The children could hear her scream all the way down until the sled bumped to a stop on the other side.

Mick and Robbie hurried down to help her bring the sled back to the top. Finally it was Dorie's turn. She had waited and waited patiently. She was both excited and nervous to see how fast the sled would go.

"Hang on a minute, Dorie, the runners need to be sharper," Mick said as they all watched him work. The sun was high in the crystal clear blue sky now. It was a warm winter day in Nebraska. "Get on, Dorie, and hang on tight."

Dorie took her place on the sled. She positioned her feet just so and grabbed onto the sides. She was ready when she felt her brothers give her a push. She soared down the snowy hill, but when the runners met the ice of the river she heard a CRACK!

Before Dorie could react, the crack in the ice gave way, spread into many cracks, and soon there was a hole gaping before her. The sled made a smooth descent into the icy water, taking Dorie with it.

"Holy mackerel," Mick exclaimed as he practically jumped from the top of the bank to the edge of the river. Marley's braid flew behind her as she ran after Mick. Robbie's short legs followed behind his brother and sister.

"Dorie, Dorie," they all screamed at once. Dorie's small head popped up along the edge of the jagged ice as she yelled, "Help me!"

Mick took charge as he assessed the dangerous situation. "Robbie, go grab some long branches from under that tree up yonder and be quick. Marley, I am going to hold on to that bush on the edge of the river bank. I will stretch out as far as I can and hold my hand out to you. You take my hand and hold on as tightly as you can. You are going to have to stretch out onto the edge of the ice, but you can do it."

Robbie was back now with some branches. His face was pale and he looked scared to death.

Dorie falls through the ice.

Mick instructed, "Robbie, you have to be tough, ya hear? Marley will hold onto your feet while you lie down on the ice. Put the branch in your hand and stretch it out over the ice to Dorie in the water. When she has it, you holler and Marley and I will pull you both back to the bank."

The complicated ballet of bodies was quickly accomplished and in a matter of seconds Dorie was pulled from the freezing river water and up onto the bank into the waiting arms of her brothers and sister.

"Mmmick, my clothes are ffffreezing uppp hhhhard as a rrrooock," Dorie chattered.

Marley cried, "What should we do now? She is going to freeze to death out here."

Mick responded rapidly, "Robbie, give me those branches you got." He pulled out a match from his pocket, arranged some dried leaves around the sticks and quickly got a fire going. "Robbie, turn your back to the girls like me," he said as he turned around with his back to the fire.

"Dorie, Robbie and I will not look. Take off those icy clothes," he commanded as he stripped off his winter coat. "Marley, wrap this around her and get her as close to the fire as you can without burning her. Call out to us when you are done."

Marley did as she was ordered even though the job was difficult. Dorie was shaking like a leaf on a tree caught in a Nebraska tornado. When she had accomplished her task she yelled at Mick. "We are ready for you."

Mick instructed Robbie to follow him as he wrapped his arms around his shivering sister. Marley and Robbie did the

Dorie dries out.

same. They turned her from side to side like a piece of meat on a campfire as she gradually thawed out in the heat of the fire and the warmth from the bundle of bodies that surrounded her.

When the crisis had passed and the children knew Dorie was all right, they decided to head back home. That was certainly enough excitement for one day. As the weary but grateful children trudged up the path toward the farm house they heard Mick cry out, "Gosh darn it, that was my sled and now it is at the bottom of the Elkhorn River!"

Dorie could not help herself. She began to laugh even though her body hurt from the cold. Robbie burst into peals of laughter at Mick's plight and even Marley began to smile and giggle. They all looked at Mick. He glowered back at them until at last he too broke into laughter over their unanticipated adventure and courageous rescue of Dorie.

Archer farm house in the winter.

The Boys of Summer

THE SINKING SUN BEAT ITS warmth down on Oakdale's dirt-covered baseball field causing waves of heat to radiate off its surface. Each summer in Nebraska was hotter and drier than the one before it. As Dorie walked toward the field she thought to herself, *This must be what the surface of the sun feels like.*

Everywhere women cooled their faces with paper fans while men took off their summer straw hats to wipe the sweat from their brows with their handkerchiefs before replacing their hats. The players from the teams facing each other were assembled on the field shagging and throwing balls to each other in preparation for tonight's game.

Mick Archer was one of the last players to take the field having put on the extra gear he wore as a catcher. As he strode onto the field, Dorie watched the girls in the stands pause in their talking and turn to look at him. It wasn't that Mick was handsome in a traditional way. No. It was more his swagger of confidence that made them turn, stare, and watch his every poised movement.

Let's play ball!

With quiet confidence he took his place behind home plate and bent his knees to play catch and throw with the pitcher. Warm-ups had started.

"Go, Mick," Dorie yelled out to him. Although Dorie would never admit it, she was proud to be his sister. From the corner of her eye she watched for the reaction of the girls in the stands as Mick waved happily back to her. Dorie enjoyed her moment of glory as the girls looked at her with jealousy and admiration.

Tonight as Dorie sat in the stands with her family, the Oakdale Antelopes were facing their arch enemy the Legion team from Tilden. It promised to be a barn burner of a game and was as hotly contested a game as any around. The stands were full with both sides cheering on their favorite team.

The contest seesawed back and forth with no advantage to either side until the top of the ninth inning when Oakdale scored their first run. Now all they had to do was hold on to their lead over Tilden and the game was over.

In the bottom of the final inning Tilden drew blood with the first batter Bubba Smith, swinging hard on a curve ball. His bat connected and sent the baseball into far left field. He swiftly hustled to second base for a double. At this point the Oakdale pitching seemed to weaken and the next batter, Hoad Newell, walked. Now two bases were filled with no outs.

Mick called time, ambled out to talk to his pitcher and attempted to calm him down. Then he took his place behind home plate. It seemed to work because the next batter struck out.

Maybe it was the extreme heat or maybe the pitcher was still shook up because the next batter sent a hard-hit ball speeding down the third base line past the glove of the third baseman. All runners advanced and now the bases were loaded with only one out.

Dorie glanced at Mick's determined face. Her confidence in him never faltered but she was a bit worried about the pitcher. She clutched her mother's hand and yelled, "Get 'em, Oakdale. You can do it!"

Tilden's next batter took his place. The pitch flew over home plate. Strike one! Dorie's spirits soared and the Oakdale crowd cheered. Mick threw the ball back to his pitcher. Dorie watched the wind up, holding her breath. To her surprise she saw the batter change the position of the bat in his hand. He was bunting! Tilden would score for sure if he made a good bunt.

Dorie watched the scene as if it were in slow motion. The bat struck the ball in a perfectly executed bunt. The ball rolled what appeared to be just the right distance forward and toward first base—not enough distance for either the pitcher or the first baseman to grab the ball.

Dorie saw a flash of movement. Mick leaped from his crouch behind the plate onto the field. He snatched the ball and in one flowing movement threw it to first base. Caught. Tilden player out!

But to everyone's surprise the first baseman flung the ball back to Mick as he moved backward to guard home plate. The Tilden runner who had been on third base was the largest player on the field. He had started to make his move and was lumbering toward home plate, prepared to score. Mick set his feet firmly and steeled his body for the impact that was to come, all the while holding the ball tightly in his glove.

Dorie and the entire crowd held their breath. The steamy night was absolutely quiet as they waited in anticipation to see who would win. The runner moved at full tilt ready to fling Mick out of the way in order to score a run. Yet Mick was aggressively blocking the base.

The collision was immense and loud. The dust flew up from the dried-out field covering the players entirely. The crowd stood on its feet to see what would happen. Would Tilden score or would it be the third out?

Dorie peered through the murky dust. As it settled she could see that there on the field lay two players—one wearing red and the other wearing blue. Clutched tightly in Mick's glove was the white baseball. The glove lay on the shoulder of the Tilden player. Inches behind Mick was home plate. Mick had stopped the Tilden player short of the base, tagged him, and got the third out!

The crowd from Tilden let out a collective groan. The Oakdale fans went wild with joy! Game over! Oakdale won, and the hero of the game was Mick Archer.

The Tilden crowd made their way out of the stands and toward home all the while reassuring themselves and the Oakdale fans that they would get them next time.

Dorie and her family dashed onto the field with the other Oakdale fans to congratulate the team. Dorie could see a strange man standing near Mick and his coach talking to them.

"Will you consider playing for our state team this year in the national tournament?" the man asked. "We need an agile and tough catcher like you. Plus there will be scouts there looking for talent to play professional baseball. Boy, you got the talent! You have a future in baseball!"

"I have to talk to my parents first," Mick replied, "but I would like to play with your team."

As Mick said these words, he looked over at Stanley who had made his way onto the field with the Archer family. Stanley nodded his head as he said, "I reckon we can spare you for a few days from the farm and your chores. Sure, you can go."

Mick smiled widely as he shook the man's offered hand. "It would be a pleasure and an honor to play for you, sir." And with that Mick walked back to the dugout unaware of the admiring stares from the crowd of girls who waited for a glimpse and maybe a chance to talk to him.

Dust, Darkness, and Danger

SPRING 1936

THE DUST THAT FILLED THE Nebraska skies most days was nothing new to the children of the red-brick one-room school house. Many days fine dust particles filled the air and blew in through the cracks in the yellowed windows of the school. A gritty film coated the desks and the floors of the school that no amount of sweeping or cleaning could ever overcome.

The children who attended the tiny school ranged in age from the five-year-old beginning learners to eighteen-year-old young men and women who were about to graduate and make their way in the world.

Everyone just learned to live and cope with the cloud of ever-present dust. In the classroom, the pages of the books felt tacky with a layer of dust. The daily turning of dust-coated pages had worn holes through the brittle books making them difficult to read and study.

But this day had dawned differently. The sun shone in the sky and the day held new hope for recovery and a better future ahead. The promise of a bright and clear spring day brought a smile to

Dorie's face. The blue sky was dotted with a few white, cottony clouds and the spring sun made a shiny, vivid appearance as the children prepared for school.

Mick, Marley, and Dorie happily picked up their books and marched toward school. It was glorious to be outside on a day with no dust! The school year would soon be over and the children would be released to their outdoor world of farm chores, swimming in the river, and the unmistakable feel of freedom only a Nebraska summer could provide. Dorie sang to herself as she walked.

Mick called to her, "Dorie, what are you so happy about today? Seems to me like walking to school is not an occasion to sing about."

Dorie smiled her answer back at him as she explained, "There have been so many dark, dusty days in a row I almost forgot what fresh air and sunlight feel like. I aim to grab onto the good days with all my might."

Dorie recalled that even Anna had seemed more hopeful this morning. As the children ate their breakfast of corn meal mush, Anna enticed them with a promise.

"We will head back to the river after you all get home from school today. We are going to have ourselves a good old-fashioned picnic on the banks of the Elkhorn. Such a gorgeous day should not be wasted indoors so hurry home from school, don't dawdle and I promise I will have everything ready." Anna's wide smile comforted the children.

Although Dorie loved school, the morning dragged on a bit as she worked on her math problems. She was distracted

Miss Hayes teaches in the one-room school house.

by the older students reading out loud. As usual, Dorie took in the words they were speaking and got caught up in the drama of the play they were reading. *Romeo and Juliet*! How Dorie loved stories!

Then, as if a witch had cast an evil spell, the wind picked up outside the school house window. Dorie could hear the mournful sound as the wind whipped around the corners of the building. Wind always brought disaster, and Dorie's senses were on high alert. Dorie peered out of the window. She could see the red dust begin to fly bringing with it the inevitable supply of tumbleweeds, which caught immediately in the fence surrounding the school yard.

Miss Hayes did not bat an eye or even flinch but continued the lesson and the reading of the play with the older students. This was nothing out of the ordinary, and although they had hoped for a beautiful day, there was nothing they could do to change the fact that the weather had turned.

Some of the younger students began to cough from time to time as the dust infiltrated their school room. The minutes ticked by. Dorie tried to concentrate on her numbers, but the wind grew stronger each passing minute. The hair on Dorie's neck began to twitch. Something was different today. Something that felt sinister to Dorie was blowing into Nebraska.

Then it happened. Slowly at first but picking up speed as the wind storm continued, the sun was obliterated by the ever deepening and inky cloud of dust. Pitch dark and more shadowy with each second, the wind stirred and poured dust over the Nebraska fields and encased the school house in murky twilight.

Alarmed, Dorie sought out Miss Hayes's face. For just a moment the calm, poised look she usually possessed disappeared but just as quickly she regained her composure. Yet Dorie could clearly read in her eyes that this swirling evil was something outside of the realm of ordinary. Dorie was frightened as Miss Hayes addressed the students.

"Sit tight," she told them. "I declare it is as dark as midnight in here. I must light our kerosene lamps to keep us working at our lessons," she explained in a determined yet guarded voice.

The anxious, silent group of students watched as she struggled to pour the kerosene into the glass base of the lamp and to light the wicks.

A kerosene lamp.

Marley boldly asked, "Miss Hayes, do you need help?"

"No, thanks, Marley, I can manage. Please stay seated until I get these lit. Then we can continue our lessons. Back to work everyone!" Miss Hayes ordered.

The children lowered their heads as if to study. Everyone pretended that everything was normal. But as they made every effort to do their work, the already sunless sky grew darker. The wind howled ominously as it lashed the dust particles into a frenzy around the red-brick corners of the building.

Dorie raised her eyes to the window. She blinked. Her eyes felt raw from the dust particles in them. She attempted to rub the dust from her eyes but rubbing only made it worse. When she was finally able to open them again, what she saw brought a lump to her throat.

There, racing toward the building, was a black wall of churning dust. It rose up into the sky hundreds of feet like one of the tall buildings she had seen in a book about New York City. Everything became dark as midnight in a cave.

"There, there," Miss Hayes comforted some of the younger children who tried to stifle the sobs of fear that leaked out. Dorie looked for Marley and Mick. *What to do?*

Dorie felt rather than saw the hand that reached out to her. Marley, seated in the desk next to Dorie, said, "Dorie, take my

Marley comforts Dorie.

hand, hold on tight. Everything will be all right. Don't worry now." Marley sought to comfort Dorie with the sound of her voice and the reassuring touch of her hand.

Thump. The sound was the only indication the children had that Miss Hayes had set her book down on the desk. The room was now pitch black. The darkness obscured even the dim light from the kerosene lamps. Nothing could penetrate the filmy, thick, dusky darkness.

Miss Hayes cleared her throat, "Children, it seems this dust just won't let go today. The darkness makes it impossible to continue school work. You must make your way home to your families. Form a line in front of me."

Dorie wondered what on earth Miss Hayes would do now. It was more difficult to breathe with each passing second. The dust covered their faces and seeped into their noses and mouths. Dorie ran her tongue over her teeth. They were coated with dirty grit. Breathing felt like fire running down her throat and into her lungs. Suddenly, Dorie heard a sound. Rip, rip, rip.

Miss Hayes directed, "Children, come toward the sound of my voice. Stand quietly in line. I have ripped these erase rags for the blackboard into swatches. I will cover your nose and mouth with the rags and tie them tightly behind your head. Be quick now."

Miss Hayes worked quietly and efficiently covering the faces of the somber children. This time she accepted the help of the older students. Mick tied rags while Marley comforted the younger children. The job was quickly accomplished.

"Now children," Miss Hayes went on, "I want each older student to grasp the hand of a younger student. You all need to

Braving the duster!

get home as quickly as possible. You must help each other. If you have a younger brother or sister here at school, find them now. Hold hands. Don't let go for anything! Make your way home. If you are alone, grab the hand of an older student. They will help you home. Keep the rags over your mouth. Use them to wipe the dust from your eyes. Don't be afraid! Be brave but go home as fast as you are able before this gets any worse."

Dorie shuddered but took a deep breath to rid her body of the fear she felt. She took Marley's hand. Marley clutched Mick's outstretched hand with her other one. With Mick leading the way, the trio stepped bravely out of the school house door and into the whirling madness of a Nebraska duster.

Mick Archer at work on the farm.

Monsters of Mayhem

SUMMER 1936

The dusters of the spring had continued into the summer. Adding more misery to the terrible weather was the heat and the lack of rain. The July sun beat down as Mick Archer worked out in the alfalfa field. Although it was only late morning, heat poured off the field and caused rivulets of sweat to stream down Mick's bare back. Stanley, standing on top of the growing haystack, was equally as hot.

Mick yelled at the horses, "Molly, Dan, pull hard!" Newly cut alfalfa had been raked into a pile on top of the long wooden rack. He watched the rack start to rise into the air loaded with the freshly cut alfalfa that would be used as feed for the animals during the winter. The rack was attached to the harnesses of Molly and Dan.

The horses seemed to know how far to pull the rack in order to deposit the alfalfa in just the right spot at the top of the stack. However, the cutting this year was nowhere near the usual amount, and Mick wondered how long this crop would last this

Stacking hay.

winter and how they would have enough to feed the animals. But some was better than none, he guessed, as he continued to work through the sweltering day.

Stanley stood atop the slowly rising stack of hay with his pitchfork in hand. He called out directions to Mick as the hay was raked into the wooden arms of the rack and the rack then raised to the top of the stack by the horses.

"Mick, place that load of hay right here," he ordered, "be exact now or this stack won't balance and it will topple over."

Mick and Stanley toiled on together while the sun baked their skin brown and the torrid Nebraska wind lashed their faces with its tendrils of heat. Each summer became more unbearable than the last. The rain the farmers depended on had not fallen this year. No rain and the intense heat had combined to produce a world-class drought in the farm fields of Nebraska. Each passing year become hotter and drier than the last, and the fields produced less yield with the crops.

After the rack reached its highest point and the hay was dumped on top, Mick paused to wipe his face with his handkerchief.

The alfalfa fields lay farthest away from the farm house. Mick and Stanley were working George Hunter's fields on this day. Their own small plot of crops nearer the farm house would have to wait until Mr. Hunter's work was done. As a hired farm hand, Stanley's first obligation was to Mr. Hunter.

From atop the hay stack his eyes surveyed the neighboring fields of corn, the green stalks whipping in the wind. Some of the stalks were already brown and would yield no corn, but at least there were some still growing. Stanley hoped they would survive until harvest so there would be at least some corn this year. Secretly he still held out hope that the rains would fall soon and save the crops.

Back at the farm house Marley and her mother were also working hard at their chores. Anna called to her daughter, "Marley, hang this laundry on the line please while I start making a lunch for Dad and Mick. They are working way out in the alfalfa field, and I know they will not want to stop and come all the way back to eat lunch. My land sakes, they need water for sure today! The laundry will dry as quick as a wink in this heat. Dorie can help you. Be sure to keep a good eye on Robbie playing out there with Jix, will you?"

Marley motioned to Dorie to grab the clothespins while she hefted the laundry basket up on her hip, and the girls went outside together. The house was located near the river so it had the great advantage of trees nearby and some shade from the sweltering sun. Even so, Dorie felt as if she had entered a blast furnace as she took her place beside her sister at the clothesline.

"Robbie, how can you stand to be outside all morning in this heat?" Dorie yelled to her brother. Robbie was engrossed in some project with his dog, Jix, and his wagon and he did not answer Dorie. She was too overheated to pursue the conversation when she heard her mother call.

"Dorie, I need you to run this basket out to the men in the field. I packed a couple sandwiches, a jar of canned peaches, and jugs of water. You can take this out to them, can't you? I need Marley to help with the rest of the chores while I tend to Maggie.

Marley hangs clothes on the line.

Robbie and Jix at play.

She has been coughing something fierce since the dust started to blow in this summer. Come quickly and get the lunch. I am sure those men are near parched to death of thirst."

Although Dorie was scorching hot, she decided a walk in the fields might be a good change of scenery. She was feeling a bit bored and cranky without school to distract her.

"Sure, Mom. I can do it with no problem. I'll be back when they are finished eating so it should not take long."

"Good girl, Dorie. I knew I could count on you," Anna smiled at her daughter, "now go on with you!"

Dorie grabbed the basket with two hands and held it tightly as she walked toward the far field. As she walked, Dorie thought about Maggie. At two years old Maggie was a frail child. Aunt Mary always said about Maggie, "She has to stand twice to make a shadow." She seemed to catch every sickness that passed through. But that was usually only in the winter. It was so strange that Maggie had a fever and was coughing ferociously in this hot summer weather.

Dorie wondered if the dust that blew in got into her tiny lungs and made it difficult for her to breathe. Sometimes even Dorie felt as if she were swallowing a mouthful of dust into her lungs. Dorie had watched as Anna doctored Maggie with a teaspoon of kerosene doused with a sprinkle of sugar to quiet her cough. There was no money for a doctor and no doctor within miles anyway, but Dorie worried that the homemade medicine was not enough. Maggie's cough grew worse every day.

With her thoughts preoccupying her mind, Dorie arrived at the field before she knew it. She called out, "Mick, Dad, come and get some lunch and a drink of water."

Their grateful faces made Dorie glad she had been the one to bring lunch out to them. The men found a bit of shade under the few trees that lined the fence line of the field. They ate and drank greedily and then lay down to rest for a few minutes in the shadow of the trees.

All too soon Stanley declared, "Time to get back to work. The sooner we work, the sooner we finish."

Dorie gathered up the empty peach jars and the wax paper wrappers from the sandwiches. The glass jugs of water were empty now, and she placed them all back in the basket. Mick and Stanley were walking toward the hay stack when they heard an unfamiliar noise.

Zzzzzzz ... the air vibrated with this unique sound. Dorie looked up to the sky to see where the noise was coming from. The blue sky that had previously been crystal clear was suddenly dark and scary looking. Was it a thunderstorm? A Nebraska tornado? Dorie fearfully looked at her father and brother. She could see their puzzled faces as they shaded their eyes to search the sky for answers.

Then it hit like a ton of bricks. The air was suddenly filled with flying insects. Grasshoppers! Thousands and thousands of grasshoppers swarmed and landed on Dorie, Stanley, Mick, and the horses.

Dorie scraped the pests from her eyes. She could see grasshoppers everywhere. They were in the trees, eating the leaves in hurried bites. She saw them on the corn stalks in the nearby field, devouring the green silky crops that were struggling to grow in the parched earth. She looked at the fence posts and

*Monsters of mayhem—the
grasshoppers arrive!*

saw hoppers gnawing the wood. There was not one inch of land where she could not see a grasshopper.

Stanley screamed as he grabbed the bridle of the horses, "Dorie, be fast, jump on Dan's back."

Dorie's face felt raw as the insects pelted her skin. She covered her mouth with her hand so the insects would not invade it as she fought to make her way to her dad. She watched as Mick grabbed Molly's bridle and slung his body onto her back. The bridle was thick with grasshoppers that seemed to thrive on the saliva that coated the leather of the horses' bits and bridles.

Dorie tried to move against the tide of invaders. The grasshoppers were the size of small birds with their wings spanning out as they flew to discover any new food source possible. As Dorie inched her way forward toward her father, she felt grasshoppers hit her chest. They pinched her skin as they dug into her.

As the hungry hoard of insects alighted on her, they spat a tobacco-like juice. Dorie desperately tried to wipe away the disgusting juice that now stained her dress but to no avail. They just kept coming and coming.

Stanley's strong, outstretched arms snatched Dorie up as he swatted the insects away from his daughter. He lifted her onto Dan's back. Stanley, already on the horse, sat behind Dorie and with a "Hiay," he sent Dan galloping back toward the farm house. Mick followed on Molly.

The three Archers and their two horses fought against the river of insects that poured over them to make their way back to the farm and barn. The effort was like swimming upstream

Stanley saves Dorie.

against the current. The skittish horses swatted the grasshoppers with their tails but made no dent in the mass of insects that hit them and landed on them. Still they fought to make their way to the barn.

Murkiness replaced the daylight although it was only early afternoon as they approached the farm yard. Dorie held on tightly to the mane of the horse as Dan carried them toward the barn.

From the corner of her eye Dorie caught sight of something white flapping in the chaos. There, standing in the middle of the throngs of grasshoppers, was Marley. She was fiercely battling the grasshoppers to retrieve the sheets from the clothesline.

Dorie could already see the holes the hoppers had eaten in the material and she cried out to Marley, " Marley, run, run to the barn. Leave those clothes and save yourself."

Hoppers covered Marley's braid, her dress, and her arms as she fought the insects over the clothing. As they neared the house they could hear Anna screaming frantically for Robbie through the open window, "Robbie, Robbie, where are you? Run fast to the house. Run to Marley! She will help you!"

Dorie's eyes searched for Robbie, Jix, and his little wagon as the horse made its way to the barn. She couldn't see them anywhere.

From behind her she could hear Mick's voice calling out to Marley, "Marley, grab my hand. You cannot stay out here. Don't worry about the clothes. Grab my hand and let me pull you up!"

Dorie's father slid off the horse and pulled open the barn door all the while swatting and hitting the pests that covered the entire door. He swatted Dan's butt to move him into the barn. Molly carrying Mick and Marley aboard followed soon after.

They were in the eye of the hurricane when they entered the barn. The safety of the barn offered a calm spot in the midst of the storm of hoppers raging outside. A few grasshoppers had entered the structure but nothing compared to the teeming mass of insects roaring outside. Dorie took her first cleansing breath, and she heard the others gulp their first breath of air without insects fighting to block their eyes, nose, and mouth.

Without warning they heard a small sob and the yelping of a dog.

"Robbie? Robbie? Are you in here?" called Stanley.

Robbie, holding onto the familiar fur of Jix, moved out of the shadow of the corner of the barn just enough for the family to see the red welts on his small, white face where he had been hit by the plague of grasshoppers.

Marley ran to him and encircled him with her arms, "Don't cry, Robbie. We are here now. It will be all right. Just sit tight and wait. Those nasty beasts will go away soon. I am sure." Marley cooed to Robbie to calm him.

Stanley stood beside the door until the roar of insects lessened. He tested the door by pushing it open slightly. A few insects entered but not the multitude they expected.

Stanley ordered the children, "Wait here until I come and get you."

"No, Dad, we're not leaving you alone," Mick said sternly. As Stanley walked from the barn the children followed behind him silently.

The family left the barn and got their first full sight of the misery that awaited them. The roving hoard of grasshoppers had indeed moved on not before eating every possible thing around. Dorie looked at the corn fields. Barely a stalk standing. Nothing left. The pests had gobbled the stalks down to the dirt. She looked at the trees. The leaves had been stripped bare. She looked at the clothes on the line. They were torn and tattered and full of holes.

Destruction was everywhere.

Stanley marched determinedly over to Mr. Hunter's truck. The children heard him mutter as if in a daze, "I gotta get over to Mr. Hunter's fields. There must be something left. It can't all be gone."

Stanley opened the door of the truck. The children watched as he swept hundreds of grasshoppers off the seat with his arm. Stanley tried to start the truck but there was no response. He got out and walked to the hood and lifted it to look at the engine. Horrified, Dorie could see it was oozing with a mass of brownish green insects.

"Children, get into the house with your mother. I aim to walk to the Hunter place to see what in tarnation is going on and just what can be saved."

The children watched their father as he made his way down the hard dirt lane that led to the highway. They listened as his shoes squished and watched as he slipped and slid over the insects left lying in the path. They saw the determination in his face as he made his way. As if in a trance of disbelief over the events of the day, the four children watched until their father's figure grew small against the now clear skyline.

It was only then they turned toward the house and wearily made their way into the waiting arms of their anxious mother.

The Chokecherry Secret

SEPTEMBER 1936

DORIE PLOPPED THE BASKET DOWN on the ground as she wiped her face. Exhausted, hot, and tired from the effort of walking from the farm house to the river, she nonetheless set about her task. The summer growing season had provided few crops and even less produce from Anna's garden. The family was always on the lookout for any food source they could find especially one that was free.

Dorie had just arrived home from her school day when she heard her mother's directions, "Dorie, dear, take this basket and head down to the river. It's time to pick chokecherries. Look for the bushes growing there that have a dark purple berry on them. You'll find clusters of berries, but make sure their color is deep, almost black.

Dorie questioned her mother, "Why should the berries be dark purple? Don't all of the berries taste the same?"

Anna was quick to respond. "The berries with the darkest color are ripe chokecherries. Now be careful, they use the word choke for a reason. If you pick the berries that are still red and ripening and put one in your mouth, you will find out why they are called chokecherries."

Dorie laughed at her mother's explanation and asked, "What will you do with the berries?"

Anna told her, "Pick as many as you find. We will use them to make jelly. If you find enough we will be able to can many jars of jelly and, God willing, that will help take us through the winter."

Dorie dutifully replied, "Sure, Mom. Can Mick or Marley come help? If one of them comes along we can carry many more baskets of berries together." Dorie did not want to shirk her duty but she also wished she could get the job done quickly and then come back home to read, play, and cool off.

Chokecherries.

"Marley needs to help me with the housework and dinner. I don't know where Mick is right now. Probably out doing his chores. Dorie, whatever you can pick will help and when you get back we will have dinner ready. Please go on now. I need your help," Anna replied.

So that is how Dorie found herself beside the river picking berries. Her weary fingers stripped the berries off the bush and plunked them into the basket. It was September but it felt like the hottest July day to Dorie. The Nebraska summer refused to give up. The heat was suffocating and intense. The sun unrelenting and together they had dried everything out. Dorie kept at her work but with the heat her fingers felt like lead. The plunk of berries hitting the bottom of the basket slowed to a crawl.

Ignoring her mother's advice Dorie decided to place just one berry in her mouth. She chose one of the darkest violet berries. After all, how bad could a berry taste? Her mother had steered her away from the red ones, but if she was going to make jelly out of the plum-colored berries, they must taste good. Dorie's lips sealed over the small berry she had just taken.

"Holy cow," Dorie's voice rang out over the river bank. The mild-looking fruit packed quite a wallop! The harsh, bitter taste of the berry made her mouth pucker so much she was unable to spit out the irritating berry. Then, suddenly, the sensation subsided and a more pleasant taste penetrated her mouth.

"Not too bad," Dorie remarked to the birds that flew around her in the trees, "don't mind if I take more of those." Dorie popped a couple more berries into her mouth.

Whoosh. A soft rustling noise caused Dorie to look away from her task and toward the river bank. Dorie felt the leaves of the trees near her swoosh and flutter as something ran past. The noise continued for a few more seconds and now Dorie could hear the thud of footsteps in the damp soil near the water's edge.

"What on earth?" Dorie said. She moved the basket nearer the bush and set off toward the sound. As she neared the bank and made her way out of the grove of trees, Dorie could see farther into the distance. It appeared to her that three figures were running. Dorie had to see what was going on. She scurried down to the edge of the water and followed the tracks the bare feet had left there.

This was much farther than Dorie had ever gone down river. And when the Cedar Creek met the Elkhorn, she saw the tracks veer off and follow the narrower creek bank. Dorie breathlessly followed until she heard the sound of voices. She stopped and knelt down behind some bushes, peering cautiously around them.

To her surprise, she saw three boys as well as a flimsy shack. The shack was perched precariously against the bank of the creek. It looked to be made from scrap pieces of wood and spare parts. Certainly not wonderful construction, yet Dorie was thrilled. She had discovered her brother's secret hideout!

"We got some and we got away," Mick's voice was jubilant. Dorie could now see Mick with his two friends, Donald and George. The three boys were in their overalls and wore no shoes. Dorie noticed the boys all looked as if they had gained twenty pounds overnight. Their overalls bulged at the seams and were pulled tightly over their chests.

George replied, "Great idea, Mick. I never knew ole man Emerson had so many watermelons in his garden. We don't have many vegetables, or anything for that matter, left in ours. He won't miss a couple of melons at all. Now let me at them. I am so hot and hungry!"

Dorie watched from behind the bush as the three boys pulled out pieces of greenish white rind with only a few pink strands of fruit attached to them. Black seeds and juice dripped over their hands. The melons had obviously been sampled. She continued to watch as the boys now reached inside their overalls and pulled out entire sections of the juicy, watery fruit. Her mouth watered. She was ready to make her move.

Dorie stepped out into the sunlight as the boys sat on the bank near the shack enjoying their stolen treats. When Mick finally took a breath from his eating frenzy and looked up, he saw Dorie standing in front of him, her arms crossed and a stubborn look on her face.

"Dorie, what in the heck? How did you find us? Where did you come from?" Mick stammered.

"You never mind about that, Mr. Mick. The jig is up! I know where you got those melons and now I know where to find your secret hideout now. What do you think Mom and Dad would say about all of this business?"

"Dorie, you wouldn't!" Mick wiped away the juice slobbering down his chin. George and Donald sat stock still but did not pause in their eating.

"You bet your buttons I would but I could be talked into making a deal to keep my silence if you are interested," Dorie bargained with Mick.

"Okay, Dorie, let me have it. What will it take to keep you from telling Mom and Dad about the melons? We only took a few. Ole man Emerson won't miss them at all," Mick reasoned.

"Hold on there. I will do the bossing here, not you," Dorie went on as she pointed her index finger at Mick. "Mom sent me down to the river to pick chokecherries for making jelly. It is hot and I am tired. I think it would be a great idea if you, George, and Donald will go finish that job for me. Then you three will carry back the basket of berries to the farm house."

"It's a deal, Dorie," Mick quickly responded.

Dorie makes a deal.

"Hold on to your horses, sir. I am not done," Dorie knew she was pushing her luck but it was worth it. "I am very hot and hungry. Give me the rest of the melons you have left. Let me sit in your hideout so I will be out of the sun and we have a deal."

Donald, George, and Mick put their heads together as if in a pow-wow. What else did they really have to bargain with? The result was inevitable.

"You got it, Dorie. But when you leave this spot you have to promise never to return. Not one word to Mom, Dad, Marley, Robbie, or even Maggie about the melons. We'll give you the biggest melon but we get the last bite of each rind."

"Deal," Dorie responded just as quickly.

Dorie sat in the cool shelter just inside the door of the shack and listened to the three boys reliving their adventure in Mr. Emerson's garden. She smiled to herself. This day had turned out much better than she thought it would. She would have the chokecherries picked for Mom, who would be happy, and she got to eat watermelon to her heart's content. Dorie filed the location of her brother's secret hideout in the back of her mind for future use.

"A good day all in all," Dorie said out loud delightedly as the sweet, sticky juice dripped down her chin.

Chokecherry Jelly

Chokecherries.

3 CUPS CHOKECHERRY
JUICE
6 1/2 CUPS SUGAR
1 BOTTLE LIQUID
FRUIT PECTIN (A BOX
OF SURE-JELL)
1/4 TEASPOON
ALMOND EXTRACT

Pour juice into a large kettle. Add sugar and stir to mix. Place over high heat and bring to a boil, stirring constantly. Stir in pectin. Bring to a full rolling boil and boil hard for one minute stirring constantly. Remove from heat. Stir and skim scum for about 5 minutes. Add extract. Pour into hot, sterilized jars. Makes 4 1/2 pints.

If you pick the chokecherries, you need to remove the stems. Cook in water, then strain the juice through a strainer or cheesecloth to get the juice. Just use enough water to cover the fruit when cooking.

You can make jelly from juice purchased in the store.

Mason jar for canning jelly.

The recipes included in this book should not be tried without adult supervision.

Duster!

THE ARCHER FAMILY HAD BECOME accustomed by now to the searing heat, the blowing wind, and the gritty sand that settled on every inch of the farm. They were even used to the grasshoppers.

In Nebraska, weather punctuated and defined the seasons. It had always been that way but this weather was different. It came, invaded, persisted, and held a strangle hold over the land, the animals, and the people. But what the Archers had not become accustomed to was the inconsistency and the whims of the dust storms, or dusters as they were now called.

There was no predicting a duster, no forewarning, no rhyme or reason as far as Dorie could tell. People just never knew when and where they would blow in or how long they would stay. So the Archers, as well as all of residents of the area of northeast Nebraska, just kept on the path of life they always had. They lived their days as they had in the years before the dusters and the hungry grasshoppers and just hoped they could outride them, outlive them, and survive them.

It was not a shock to Dorie to wake up as the darkness of the night was giving way to the dawning skies of the day, the lightening of the dark black night sky into the pale pink and gray streaks of an early morning dawn in Nebraska.

Dorie lay in her bed, her senses on high alert. Something was different. She could hear the soft rhythmic breathing of Marley and the restless rustling of Maggie in her narrow bed. Dorie remained still and quiet.

The roar came slowly as the wind picked up in intensity. Dorie peered out of the bedroom window. Although the transformation of night to dawn blocked her view slightly, she knew what was happening outside.

She could hear the gritty sand beginning to blast against the frame of the farm house with its incessant beat as the mournful wind moaned and whistled outside. Faster now it whipped its frenzy of dust into clouds that encircled the farm house and fields.

Dorie hurried back to her bed and scrunched down under the blanket. She covered her ears with her hands to escape the awful sound of the roaring tempest. Dorie likened her situation to being inside an imaginary box where she was trapped by the swirling dust that lashed out at the Archer farm.

Dorie was in a jail created and maintained by the elements of wind and dust. There was no escape. She felt scared, tiny, alone, and powerless to fight the fury of the gigantic duster that was rolling through. Tears fell onto her cheeks as she fought the rising tide of fear. She whispered a prayer she learned at church, "Our Father who art in Heaven …"

Dorie looks over the devastation of the duster.

The duster lasted for what seemed like hours although judging by the sky it was no more than a few minutes. Dorie popped her head up from under the covers. Marley and Maggie were still asleep and, for a second, Dorie wondered whether she had dreamed the storm. Then she looked out the window.

She could see someone in the corn field nearest the house. Dorie slipped her feet in her shoes and pulled a robe over her pajamas. Cautiously she went down the stairs and opened the front door. She knew now. It was her father out in the field.

Impulsively Dorie ran out of the house. She ran through the farm yard and headed to the field without calling out and in complete silence. She was scared and she wanted her father to grab her up into his strong arms and reassure her that everything was all right.

Stanley was kneeling in the field. Jix was by his side as Dorie approached them. Dorie smiled at the familiar figures of her father and the family pet but then raised her gaze to take in the field of corn.

Yesterday the field, although dry, was beginning to show signs of green stalks of corn growing. Some of the corn they planted had not made it, the edges of the field showed brown and stubby stalks that would yield no corn, but there was some life there, a start, a way to feed the cattle, and a beginning of the food the family would eat for the next winter.

Dorie drew her breath in sharply as she looked over the field today. The stalks had been blasted by the sharp and cutting wind carrying the dust. It was as if a machine had cut a jagged swath through the corn. What had been green and growing stalks were cut off in a ragged line, mowed down by the driving force of wind and dust.

Dorie moved quietly toward her father. Dorie would never forget what happened next. Neither Stanley nor Jix felt Dorie's approach. She could hear Jix whimpering softly. She looked at her father's face as his hand petted the silky fur of the dog, rhythmically moving his hand over and over his back. Tears ran down his cheeks and he soundlessly grieved over his lost crop.

Dorie choked back a sob as she felt the last particles of dust scrape her face. She felt raw but she didn't know if it was the dust or the fear she felt as she watched her father wordlessly cry.

In a whisper of a voice Dorie called, "Dad."

Just that one word. She saw Stanley wipe his cheeks off with the back of his hand, gather himself together, and turn toward her voice.

He did not say a word but instead held his hand out to Dorie who grasped it tightly. Dorie, Stanley, and Jix knealt in the stale, dusty dawn. Dorie stood behind them. The heat of the day had already begun to radiate over the farm. They watched together as the sun continued its relentless task of baking the already parched and devastated land.

The Archers grieve over the lost crops.

Runners and Clean Up

LATE SUMMER 1937

THE SUFFOCATING HEAT THAT ENVELOPED the Archer home had driven all of the children outside, searching for some relief. Fortunately, there was a hint of a breeze today and the best news was that the breeze carried no dust.

Mick, of course, was off helping his father with farm work. Marley, Dorie, and Maggie read and rested under the shade of the oak trees that lined the road.

Robbie stepped out of the outhouse, which was located just behind the farm house. He walked down the well-worn path. There was no indoor plumbing inside the farm house so the outhouse served as the only toilet for the family. It was a much more enjoyable experience to use the outhouse in the warmer weather than it was when winter's grip caused the outhouse to be filled with snow and ice.

Robbie pulled the straps of his overalls up and snapped them in place on his shoulders. "Hey, girls," he called out to them, "how about a race?"

Looking up from the pages of her book Dorie quizzed him, "What do you have in mind, Robbie?"

"How about a race of runners? We can set up an obstacle course and then see who wins?" Robbie proposed.

"You're on!" Dorie replied quickly. "I'm up first. Then the winner takes on the next challenger."

Dorie and Robbie gathered up the sticks and wheels needed to play the game while Marley and Maggie set up an obstacle course. The two racers took their place at the starting line.

"Get ready, get set, go!" Marley yelled to Dorie and Robbie while three-year-old Maggie stood at her side eagerly waiting for the race to start.

"ROBBIE, that's cheating," Dorie screamed as Robbie's left arm shot out and gave Dorie a shove to push her off course.

The children were lined up on the hard trodden dirt road that led from the highway to the farm house. It was little more than a path but it led around the farm house and was definitely wide enough for the game the children played today.

Runners was one of their favorite games. There certainly was no money for store-bought toys, but the Archer children didn't need any of that fancy stuff when they could use their own imaginations. Mick had constructed the game from Robbie's idea.

First, Mick took the heavy metal inside of an ancient wagon wheel that had seen better days. Mick found two old, narrow boards in the corner of the barn. He didn't know where they had come from or what they had been used for but it didn't appear as if anyone would miss them. He nailed the shorter board securely onto the longer board and only a few inches from the bottom.

Dorie and Robbie
play runners.

The long board was about three inches wide, just enough width for the wagon wheel to slide down and begin its race onto the dirt course they had designed around the house.

The purpose of the shorter board near the bottom was to "steer" the wagon wheel in the direction the racer desired. The children had set out branches as obstacles on the course. The idea was to steer their wagon wheel around the course, all of the obstacles, and arrive at the finish line first. But that was easier said than done.

The weight of the wagon wheel caused it to fly down the stick, onto the dirt road and roll in every which direction unless the racer was very fast and skillfully directed the wheel with the stick, which they held in their hands.

"Ouch," Robbie cried as Dorie gave him a swift kick to the leg and took off behind her wheel. Dorie's feet practically flew off the dirt road causing wisps of dust to rise in the air. She was nearing the growing shelter belt of trees that the family had planted a couple summers ago. The trees were not big yet but when they reached full height they would provide a wonderful barrier from the wind for the farm house. People were always trying to out think the dust!

Dorie concentrated on making the turn around the farm house to keep ahead of Robbie.

"I'll get you, Dorie," she heard Robbie's voice call to her from behind. And sure enough with each passing second she could hear the *thud, thud, thud* of his footsteps get nearer and nearer to her. She pushed herself to go faster all the while guiding the wheel with her stick.

Suddenly, from the corner of her eye, she saw a wagon wheel whirr past her. Following closely behind was a stick and holding the stick was her brother. Dorie had never seen Robbie move that fast except, of course, to get to the dinner table.

"ARRGGHHH," Robbie gave a last exertion as he glided smoothly in front of Dorie. Marley and Maggie stood just a few feet in front of them holding a rope between them. The girls pulled the rope taut to serve as a finish line

"The finish line, victory is mine," roared Robbie as he hit the rope with his waist and fell exhausted onto the dirt road. Dorie was bent forward trying to catch Robbie but her effort was just too little, too late.

"You beat me fair and square, Robbie," Dorie told him, "but I'll get you next time." Dorie's face shone with sweat as she slumped to the earth to rest with Robbie.

"Childreeeennnn," a voice called from the house, "bath time!" Anna's voice rang out over the farm yard heat. It was nearing dusk on this summer Saturday night. The Archer children were well aware of the ritual that was to come.

"*Clunk, clunk, clunk,*" the noise of the tin wash tub being pulled up the front porch stairs rang out into the dusty Nebraska air.

"C'mon you three," Marley ordered her siblings in a gentle yet firm voice. "Let's go and get this over with. Mother does not like to wait."

The four children shuffled up to the porch and into the house. The summer air was stifling inside the kitchen. Anna had been baking today. Although the bread smelled delicious the heat from the oven of the wood stove made the kitchen a sweltering inferno.

Anna wiped her hair back from her steamy face as she pulled the tub near the stove. It did not matter which season it was, the tub was always placed in the same location. The area near the stove felt much better in January, with winter's icy fingers reaching in through the cracked kitchen windows to chill the bathing children, than it did in July. But order was order and that was the location for the tub.

Anna made her way outside to the well where she pumped enough water to fill the bucket. She carried the bucket inside and when she saw the children gathered there she instructed them, "Robbie, take this bucket. Dorie you grab the other one and fill them from the well. Hurry now because I need to get all of you children bathed before we leave for town."

Robbie and Dorie did as they were told only stopping for a few extra seconds to take a long drink of the cold well water. They were thirsty from their game of runners, and this was their chance to drink in as much cool water as their stomachs could hold.

They lugged the buckets back up the stairs and into the kitchen. Anna poured them into the tub and sent the children back for more. This process was repeated several times until Anna felt the tub was sufficiently full. Then Anna dipped into the reservoir on the side of the wood stove to fill a bucket with water. At least, this water provided, some warm water for the children.

Stanley quipped good naturedly to Anna, "You are gonna spoil those children heating up that water."

Bath time.

Anna watched as Stanley stood in the entry way of the farm house removing his boots. She replied, "That is a small comfort I can give them, Stanley, and I am going to keep doing it! I know they appreciate it much more in January than they do in July."

Anna had gathered towels, soap, and clean underwear for each of the four children. Mick had been out in the fields with his father all day, and Anna knew he would take care of his own bath by dipping his overheated body into the Elkhorn River for a wash.

"All right, you children get ready now. You know the order. Marley, you are the oldest so you go first and you get to go alone.

Don't take too long in there though. The other children need to bathe too, and I don't want the water to get too cold," Anna said.

Marley popped into the tub first, scrubbing her body and washing her long hair while the other children waited their turn. Being the oldest was an advantage at bath time but Marley didn't push her luck. She finished quickly, wrapped the towel around her body, took the clean clothes Anna had set out and finished dressing upstairs in the girls' bedroom.

"You're next, Dorie, but please take Maggie in with you. You can help her wash her hair and that way the water won't get too cold by the time it gets to her," Anna told them.

Dorie was used to this arrangement. Before Maggie was old enough to bathe with her, Dorie had bathed with Marley this way. They all had to use the same water, so two in the tub was a good idea. Maggie played and splashed in the water as Dorie quickly washed the sweat away from her hair and body. When she was finished, Dorie set about helping Maggie.

"Hold still, Maggie, you are like a jumping bean," Dorie laughed as she attempted to corral and wash her sister. The girls finished their task, got out of the tub, and wrapped up in the towels to go to their room and dress.

"You're up, Robbie," Anna yelled to him. Robbie was not smiling as he looked at the murky, and just a bit dingy, bath water.

"Why do I have to go last?" Robbie whined to his mother.

"Oh, Robbie, it has been a long, hot day. Just get in the tub and wash up. The sooner you get in, the sooner you get out. Then we will load up and go to town to sell the eggs and the butter I made today. Maybe we will have a penny for some candy for you. I promise you can be the first to choose," Anna bribed him.

Robbie's face perked up a little with the enticement of candy. He bathed rapidly and was dry and dressed before the girls had their hair done.

"I'll wait for you outside," Robbie called to the girls as he walked out the door.

The Saturday night trip to town was always exciting for the children. The girls buzzed with laughter talking about what they might do when they got to town. Anna sighed. She was tired but she still had some work to do to get the family, the items they would sell, and herself into the wagon.

"I better get ready too," Anna said out loud. She took off her apron and hung it on the hook on the kitchen wall. Her hands smoothed out the only dress she owned so it looked neat. She ran her hands through her hair once and made sure her shoes were fastened tightly.

Anna grabbed the basket of eggs she was taking to Taylor's grocery store. She would barter with these eggs and the butter they churned themselves for items the family needed but had no money to buy, such as flour and sugar.

"Girls, come on now. Your father and Mick have the wagon ready. Molly and Dan don't like to be kept waiting so let's get going," she called to the voices upstairs. Anna put her hat on her head, the egg basket resting on her arm, and walked to the waiting wagon.

With everyone loaded in the wagon, the Archers set off down the road toward

The butter churn.

town. The horses pulled the wagon easily on the flat road. But as they began their ascent of the hill that would take them into town, Dan slowed his pace. Molly strained and pulled harder to get the wagon up over the hill, but Dan seemed to have developed a case of laziness as he lagged behind Molly's lead.

Stanley clicked his tongue at the horses and shook the reins. Then they heard it. "Fffrrppttptp, purtttt."

"What on earth is that loud noise?" Anna questioned her husband.

Marley called out, "And what is that terrible stench?"

Mick and Robbie were already doubled over with laughter. Stanley had a sly grin on his face. Mick blurted out, "Girls, girls, girls, don't you know a fart when you hear one? Dan has gas something fierce today."

"Well, I declare, that is just plain awful!" Marley replied.

But as soon as the words were out of her mouth, the entire Archer family could not contain themselves any longer, and they fell into peals of laughter. Dan looked back at them, his face innocent as he continued his slow, gassy climb up the hill as the Archer family reveled in the joke at Dan's expense.

Molly and Dan pull the Archer family wagon to town.

Fight Back, Maggie!

LATE FALL 1937

INDIAN SUMMER WAS WHAT FOLKS called an unusually warm autumn season in Nebraska. Dorie thought they should just drop the Indian and call it summer because this fall was as hot as any summer season she had ever known.

Dorie had finished her school day and was walking down the dirt road that led home. Her day at school had gone well but her heart was full of anxiety. Dorie had been awake for much of the night. She lay, listening for Maggie's breathing. Maggie had been fighting this strange sickness for over a year now.

Each day Maggie struggled to breathe. Her cough was ferocious and persistent. Her fever raged and subsided and then broke out and raged again the next week. Maggie spent most of her days lying on the sofa. It broke Dorie's heart to see that small, sickly bundle shivering under a blanket when the day was blazing hot.

Dorie's sorrow increased when she heard Maggie say, "Mom, it hurts." And there was nothing Dorie or anyone else could do to help.

It was common knowledge now that the small particles of dust that arrived with the dusters got into people's lungs, clogging and choking their breathing. It hit the children and the elderly especially hard. There had been reports of deaths in the next county.

Anna kept a vigil over Maggie, doctoring her the best way she knew how. When Maggie's fever rose and her cheeks shone bright red, Anna would give Maggie a sponge bath, trying her best to cool Maggie's fever and make her comfortable. When Maggie complained about her chest hurting, Anna would make a chest plaster from kerosene and lard to rub on Maggie's small frame. She hoped this would relieve her cough and lung congestion.

Homemade cough syrup of kerosene and sugar.

As soon as Dorie entered the house, she could tell that things were getting worse. Anna directed her immediately, "Dorie, please go get the petroleum jelly. Maybe if I can coat inside Maggie's nose, it will catch the dust and stop it from getting into her lungs. And, Dorie, please grab more kerosene. It is time to give Maggie another dose of our homemade cough syrup. Poor thing!"

Maggie's breath came in ragged and erratic puffs. Clearly she was suffering more now than this morning, her racking cough filled the room with a terrifying noise.

[Editor's note: Kerosene is a poison. Do not eat or drink kerosene. This home remedy was used a long time ago and should never be tried today.]

Dorie quickly gathered the items her mother requested and returned to the front room. She watched as her mother applied the Vaseline to Maggie's nose and delivered a spoonful of the homemade cough medicine made of kerosene and sugar to Maggie's tired mouth.

"There now, Maggie, you rest. Dorie is here to keep you company. She will read your favorite story to you. Just get better, Maggie, just get better," Anna pleaded with her tiny four-year-old daughter.

The Archer children were fortunate to have a few books of their own. These books had been given to them by their grandmother. Dorie hurried to grab Maggie's favorite book, *The Little Engine That Could*, from the shelf. She read slowly and carefully to the sick girl trying her best to interest her in the pictures.

"I think I can, I think I can," Dorie read aloud.

Maggie listened but her tired eyes could not stay open. Gradually they fluttered in between sleep and wakefulness as Dorie read on. When Dorie finished, she looked over at Maggie who smiled weakly. Maggie's small voice reached out to Dorie as she whispered the words of her most treasured story, "I think I can, I think I can."

Dorie's heart broke all over again. She took Maggie's small, hot hand in hers, leaned over and said, "You can, you can, Maggie. Fight back hard!"

With those words Maggie closed her eyes as her sister silently stroked her hand.

I think I can, I think I can!

The Best Choice

DORIE PRIED HER FREEZING EYELIDS open and stretched her legs and moved her feet seeking any remnant of warmth that remained under the hand-sewn quilt her grandmother had made. In the next bed Marley was sound asleep. Her breathing was regular and strong. In the other bed Maggie was also sleeping soundly. She had been without a fever for a few weeks and was slowly improving although her breathing was often labored and difficult.

The night before, Anna had heated the iron by placing it on the wood-burning stove in the kitchen. She kept it there until it was red hot. Then she carefully wrapped a blanket securely around the iron tucking in the edges and tying knots in them to preserve the heat of the iron and in order not to burn Dorie's feet. As Anna tucked Dorie into bed, she had placed the covered iron near the foot of Dorie's small iron-framed bed.

"Sleep tightly, little one," Anna murmured softly as she closed the bedroom door.

Dorie's frosty morning.

During the night Dorie had been awakened by the forlorn howling of the wind. The gusts caused the branches of an ancient oak tree to creak against the house awakening Dorie's worst fears of the darkness.

Anna's iron.

Dorie buried her head under the covers and inhaled the remainder of the warmth inside her cottony cocoon. She closed her eyes, willed herself to ignore the wind, and put herself back to sleep by thinking of green fields on a perfect spring day, creamy milk still warm and straight from the cow, freshly cooked cobs of yellow corn slippery with thick melting butter, and the soft reassuring feel of Jix's fur.

Dorie blinked her eyes back to the morning. She looked at the lacey patterns of ice that had formed on her windows during the night. She could still hear the wind blowing and now that wind was visible by the tiny white puffs of snow that entered her room through the spaces around the window sill.

She turned over on her back, sat upright, and gasped from the icy cold air that entered her lungs. A thin layer of frost coated the threadbare hand-me-down quilt on her bed.

Dorie knew that comfort and warmth would only come from the kitchen downstairs and its centerpiece, the large black wood stove.

Dorie willed her body out of bed, grabbed her robe from the foot of the bed, her wool socks covering her feet as she scurried down the wooden steps toward the kitchen and the warmth of both the stove and her family.

The wood-burning stove.

Dorie sensed rather than saw that something was not right. She stopped near the bottom of the steps just short of the entrance to the kitchen. Stanley and Anna were already seated at the table. Their heads were bent toward each other, and they were speaking in hushed tones.

A sudden movement drew Dorie's attention away from her parents as she saw Mick move toward the stove, grab the coffee pot, and pour some of the steaming liquid into his cup. A Western Union telegram lay in the middle of the table, but it was too far away for Dorie to read.

"That's it. That's all there is. My mind is made up and there is nothing else to talk about," Mick stated plainly. "I am staying here and I am not going back to the baseball team when I know plain and simple how much you need my help here at the farm."

"But, Mick," Anna pleaded, "this is your only chance and it is a big one for you. You could make the big leagues if you keep traveling and playing with the team. Your dad and I do not want you to give up on your dream."

"I will hear no more. Enough," Mick abruptly cut Anna off. "I said my mind is made up. I already talked to Joe over at the sale barn. They need men to drive the cattle truck to Omaha. They don't know for sure just when a load will go so they need men who can come and go at a moment's notice. It's much harder for the married men with families so I fit the bill just perfectly. I will go round and let everyone in these parts know that I can work whenever someone might need some help. I can fix anything, lift anything, ride and rope, and farm anything they can throw at me. The money I make doing these jobs will help around here, and we will be all right. We will get by together."

Stanley's shoulders seemed to sag a little bit further down. He put his

A Western Union telegram was one of the few means of communication in the 1930s.

head in his hands but did not say a word. He simply gave a huge, bone-tired sigh.

Stanley had been working for the government program, the WPA or Works Progress Administration, since the grasshoppers had destroyed their crops. President Franklin Roosevelt, whom everyone called just FDR, wanted to help out the farmers so he had formed this program that provided work for the farmers who had no work at all.

The WPA had been building bridges and roads, and the money Stanley made kept the Archers afloat. But now so many farmers needed the work, the WPA had to limit the hours each man could work in order to spread the jobs around. There would be even less money coming in now, and it would have to cover an already stretched tight budget.

"Son, I can't let you make a choice to give up on your opportunity to play professional baseball," Stanley's soft voice was not much above a whisper.

"Dad, it's not your choice to make. It is mine and I choose the Archer family over baseball any old day," Mick grinned at his father.

Anna's lips hovered somewhere between a smile and sob as she gazed proudly at her son. "Mick, we are grateful for your help. We do need you but we love you even more. We are proud of the man you have become," Anna said as she grasped Mick's hand.

Mick sat down at the table and placed his coffee cup in front of him. Without a word he slowly stretched out his other hand and grasped Stanley's hand. Mother, father, and son sat silently together contemplating the future and just how they would get through it.

Dorie blinked back tears. At that instant her mind took a picture she would never forget. Three of the most important people in her life sat at the table on that snowy, cold winter day, banding together to make and sustain a future for the Archer family.

A family united.

The Wonder of Bread

FEBRUARY 1938

THE ICY WIND BLEW SKIFFS of snow over the highway. Mick Archer kept his eyes peeled on the road as he drove the cattle truck back to Oakdale. He had dropped off a load of cattle at the sale barn in Omaha. Mick was pleased as punch to have this job, and although it was not steady work it was paying work nonetheless. He could help out the family with the money he earned and get to see the big city at the same time.

Mick had to concentrate as he kept the truck moving down the highway. There were not many vehicles out and about on this cold, snowy evening. Every so often Mick would pass a vehicle traveling in the opposite direction. Each driver would wave a greeting to the other as they journeyed to their destinations on this freezing night.

As Mick neared Fremont, about twenty miles from Omaha and with nearly one hundred miles to go to Oakdale, he could make out a dark object up ahead in the middle of the road. The outline of the object was silhouetted against the white snow that blew over the road.

Mick drives the truck.

"What in the sam hill?" Mick said out loud as he applied the brakes to the truck. He stopped short of the object and pulled over to the side of the road. He was aware that anyone following him might not be able to see him clearly. He did not want to cause an accident. He also knew he must remove the object from the road to avoid further danger to drivers who may not see it in time.

Mick opened the door and jumped down quickly. His overall-covered figure stood stock still for a few seconds as he looked to the right and then to the left for any traffic.

"No one is out tonight that don't have to be," he declared.

Mick quickly made his way over to the object. He could see now that it was a very large cardboard box. He put his arms around the box and tugged. He didn't know what was inside, but it was fairly light. With the box secured in his arms, he made his way back to the truck. He easily tossed the box into the truck bed, jumped up, and took out his hunting knife. He sliced through the sealed box and opened the flaps.

"Mercy me," Mick exclaimed as he peered inside. "This box is plum full of store-bought Wonder Bread!"

Mick looked up and down the road for the delivery truck he was sure had been carrying the boxes of bread. He thought maybe he could catch up to the truck and let them know their precious cargo had fallen off.

Mick started up the truck and took off, traveling faster than he usually drove. He kept alert for any vehicle he might see, even one by the side of the road as he made his way toward Oakdale. He still thought he might catch the delivery truck before it was too late.

The stiff wind had picked up its pace and the snow was coming down harder. Mick drove on through the night all the while on the lookout. But secretly inside he hoped he would never find the truck. What at treat this bread would be for his family!

Mick's secret wish was realized as he eased the truck down the dirt road to the house. The snow was piled up several inches now and he was relieved to be home—with a surprise.

Mick grabbed the box and walked toward the door. As he pushed it open he shouted, "Come and see what I brought you all from Omaha."

That was all it took. In an instant, Marley, Anna, Dorie, Robbie, and even Maggie surrounded him.

"What's in the box, Mick? Is it for us? Where did you get it?" A chorus of voices rose up around him.

"Now I know Dad is out doing chores but I can't wait to show you," Mick said as he flung open the flaps of the box.

"Glory be," Anna muttered. "Mick, where did you get the money to buy this much bread?"

"That's the best part, Mom," Mick explained to her. "I was driving along when I came upon this box in the road. I looked and looked for the delivery truck, but on this snowy night who knows where that truck went. So, not finding the truck, I decided this bread was meant for us!"

His explanation wouldn't have mattered anyway because the hungry children had already torn into the box filled with loaves of wrapped bread. Robbie was stuffing bread into his mouth as quickly as he grabbed it from the wrapper. Dorie was not far behind him all the while Marley lectured about going to the table to eat while Maggie stood gaping in wonder at all of them.

"Mick, thank you, thank you, thank you!" Dorie cried out for all of them. "I am pretty sure I just died because this must be what heaven looks like."

Mick sat and smiled. He watched as his siblings and mother took the box to the kitchen to unload, happy to have the bread to eat for the next few days. He marveled at the vast amount of wonder a box of bread could bring.

The wonder of bread.

The Shoe That Did Not Cooperate

SPRING 1938

"DORIE," ANNA CALLED TO HER middle daughter. "Time for dinner."

Dorie was sitting on the staircase enjoying the fresh spring breeze that blew in from the open bedroom window. This was one of those exceptional days when the sky was blue, the clouds white and cottony, and there was no dust.

Dorie leaned her head against the oak banister and thought about her new problem. She sighed and called back to her mother, "Coming, Mom, just a few minutes." Dorie needed a few moments of solitude, some time to think, before the hustle and bustle of her family dinner hour.

Marley was busily setting the table. She pulled the glasses from the cupboard and turned them right side up. When Anna washed and dried her dishes, she placed the glasses and the plates upside down in the cupboard. This would save her from washing them again. When the dust blew in, the upside-down dishes would be protected from the film that covered everything and they could be easily used for meals. Marley moved efficiently about the table.

Anna took their nightly dinner from the stove. Tonight she had prepared mush and milk again just like they had eaten so many other nights. The corn meal mush bubbled and popped in the bowls as they poured the milk, fresh from their cow, over the hot mixture.

After dinner Anna would pour the left-over mush into a pan. She would allow the pan to sit out overnight. The mush would harden by the morning. Then she would slice it into portions for each of them and fry it in oil. This would be dinner for the next night. If they were lucky there might be some sugar to sprinkle over the fried corn meal mush to sweeten the taste and maybe a bit of rich butter.

Dorie was tired of corn meal mush but she did not complain. It was food, it was hot, and they had something to eat. Anna worked so hard to make interesting meals out of the food they had. When they were fortunate to butcher a pig, she rendered the fat to make lard and cracklings. They spread the lard on bread and took it in their school lunches. The cracklings were the crispy and deliciously salty remains of the rendered pig fat. They provided nutrition and taste.

Nothing was wasted from the butchered pork. The left-over fat was then cooked and used to make soap. Anna poured lye into the cooking batter of fat and skimmed the white compound off the top of the concoction. She let this harden and then cut it into bars that the family used as soap and also for washing clothes.

Anna remakes a dress.

It never ceased to amaze Dorie the magic her mother could make! She was always creating something out of nothing for her family.

As the meal ended, Anna said to the girls, "Marley, bring that old dress to the kitchen. You know the red cotton one that is too small for you. Dorie come and stand over here on this chair. The dress is too big for you but I can fix that."

Marley brought the well-worn dress to the kitchen and handed it to her mother. Dorie put the frock on over her clothes. Anna immediately set to work. "We can make this into a new summer dress for you, Dorie. I will add some lace to the collar and you will look like a million dollars."

Anna smiled as she tore into the sleeves and seams of the dress. She placed her straight pins in her mouth. As she worked at raising the hem of the dress, she extracted a pin from her mouth to mark the new hem line. She worked her way around the dress until all of the pins in her mouth were gone.

"Thank you," Dorie replied weakly to her mother.

"Now, Dorie," Anna quit working to look in her daughter's eyes. "What on earth is the matter with you tonight?'

Dorie looked at the floor and her eyes filled with tears. She did not want to give her mother another problem. Anna already had so many! But she couldn't hide this from her. Mother had always told her to do your best at school you needed to look your best.

"Go on now, Dorie," Anna said gently, "do tell me what is bothering you."

"Well," Dorie started slowly, "remember when the sole of my shoe wore through and there were holes with my socks peeking through?"

"Yes, dear," Anna quietly and patiently replied. "Dad fixed that by tacking a piece of cardboard onto the bottom of your shoe. He did a good job of making it fit perfectly."

Dorie's downcast look told Anna there was more to the story. "Dad did a great job but yesterday another hole wore through," Dorie reported sadly.

"Dorie, that is not a problem and if that is the worst thing that ever happens to you, then you will be lucky. We will go right now and Dad can tack a new cardboard sole onto that shoe. We will shine them up and make them look brand new, all ready for school tomorrow."

Dorie's face brightened a little. She happily watched as her father tacked some small nails into the bottom of the newly cut cardboard. She pushed her foot into the shoe, walked back and forth a few times, and pronounced it good as new.

"See there, Dorie," Stanley lectured her, "there is no problem too big to solve if we just work together. There is always a solution to your problems. Don't ever forget that."

Spring in Nebraska could be unpredictable. One day could dawn bright, sunny, and hot and the next day the temperature could hover just above freezing, so Dorie was not surprised when she awoke to some cold weather the next day. She ate her breakfast and prepared for the walk to school by placing some extra newspaper inside her shoes to help warm her feet. She checked the newly repaired sole. Everything was fine and Dorie, sure now that she looked her best, was ready to do her best.

With Mick at work, now Marley, Dorie, and Robbie trudged down the road to school. The Nebraska wind had risen during the night and a cold breeze brought a rosy color to Dorie's cheeks.

Dorie had walked about a mile when she first began to notice a problem. First she noticed her right foot felt colder than her left foot. She walked a bit farther before she started to hear a thump, thump, thump sound. Trying to be inconspicuous, she looked down as she turned the bottom of her right shoe up to take a look.

"Oh no," Dorie noiselessly murmured. The cardboard fix of her shoe was beginning to flap loose just a bit. Dorie could see the sole was missing a few of the small nails her father had pounded in last night.

There is no problem I cannot solve, Dorie repeated over and over. Reassured by her courage she bravely kept the pace toward the school house.

As the morning progressed Dorie took her place at the chalk board with the other students who were studying the same math problems as she was—multiplication and division. She concentrated on her practice, but when she finished and started to return to her seat she felt the sole of her shoe flap even more loosely against the wooden floor of the school. Dorie hung her head as she hurried to her desk trying to muffle the noise.

What to do, what to do? Dorie thought. She was both scared and embarrassed to think someone might notice her flapping sole. To do your best, dress your best. Dorie placed her foot with the wobbly sole securely under her other foot in order to hide her shoe from the eyes of the other students.

"Recess," called Miss Hayes.

Dorie usually loved recess. It was a time to play some games and be outside in the fresh air. But not today. What was she going to do? How could she hide her sloppy shoe from the others?

"Dorie, come play jump rope with us," Emmer called to her.

"Not today, Emmer," Dorie yelled back. "I just want to sit for a while today. I am tired." Dorie observed the other children divide up into favorite games as she sat in the cool sunshine of the spring day. Some boys started a baseball game over in the far corner of the school yard. Some of the girls jumped rope, while others sat on the teeter totter.

Dorie watched sadly as some of the children divided up into her favorite game of Ante I Over. The teams today divided up along male and female lines. The team of girls went to one side of the red-brick school house and the boys took their place on the other side. As the strongest boy tossed the ball over the slanted roof of the school, his team yelled out, "Ante I Over!"

Dorie had to giggle a bit because now, when she was not playing the game, she listened carefully to the words. It sounded just like *aunty - eye - over* to her, and she smiled at her discovery.

The girls on the other side were ready. If one of the girls did not catch the ball, they would have to throw it back over calling out the same, "Ante I Over!" with no hope of capturing a boy for their team.

But today Naddie caught the ball and immediately the girls took off to the other side to tag a slow boy by throwing the ball at the chosen victim. If a boy was hit with the ball, he then was required to join the girls' team. A terrible disgrace!

The girls, with the tagged boy, would return to their side. Now it was the girls' turn to throw the ball over and try to evade the boys' tagging. The game would continue this way until no one was left on one side.

"Smack." Dorie's focus had been on the Ante I Over game, but from out of the blue something hit Dorie hard on the side of head. She fell backward from the blow. All of the children rushed over to see what happened and help her.

Sam said, "Dorie, I am so sorry. I hit that baseball a little too hard and it veered over to you. I am sorry it hit you. Are you all right?"

The girls pulled Dorie up to her feet, brushed off her dress, and began to walk her over to the steps of the school so she could sit in the shade protected from the wind. Marian ran to the well to get a drink of water for her.

Dorie walked on unsteady legs toward the building with the girls holding her arms. She looked down at her shoe. The left shoe was just fine but somehow the right one had disintegrated, and Dorie was standing in the school yard wearing a completely bottomless shoe.

Dorie had no choice. Her mother would be angry if she ruined her only pair of socks by walking on the dirt- and gravel-covered yard. She took her shoe off, held it in her hands, and began to cry.

"Dorie, don't cry," Marian begged as she handed the water to Dorie that she had just gotten from the well. She encircled Dorie with her arms as the children stood together in the school yard.

The uncooperative shoe.

"I am so ashamed," Dorie whispered. "I want to dress my best to do my best but my shoe just did not cooperate."

Marian giggled at Dorie's comment, "Oh, Dorie, look around. We are all in the same boat as you. Haven't you noticed that Sam is wearing shoes at least two sizes too big for him? He stuffs newspaper in the toes to keep his feet in them. He has to wear his brother's old shoes and they just don't fit him yet. Look at me, Dorie. Did you notice this blouse is made from the feed sacks our dads use?"

"Look at my sister, Cheetie, over there," Betty said. "Here is a secret. I can tell you that her underwear is made from a flour sack, and if you saw her bottom you would see the colored words from the sack have worn off onto her skin and you could read the words, *My Kind Of Flour*. Dorie, we are all making do with what we have. Your shoe falling apart is nothing new to any of us. It could happen to one of us in the blink of an eye."

Dorie looked into the faces of her school mates. They were right. Mother was right. If a shoe falling apart was the worst thing that happened to her, well then she was a lucky girl.

Flour sack underwear.

"Come on, Dorie. Let's go show Miss Hayes. She is one smart teacher and I bet she will have a solution for us," Marian ordered.

Dorie wasn't happy about the shoe, but she turned to the door of the school house knowing she was surrounded by people who understood how to cope with problems and get by. Dorie would never feel sorry for herself again, she resolved, instead she would look for ways to help others learn to get by with the materials and the brains the good Lord gave them.

The wood-burning stove.

Corn Meal Mush

2 CUPS CORN MEAL
2 CUPS COLD WATER
2 1/2 TO 3 CUPS BOILING WATER
3 TEASPOONS SALT

Mix corn meal and cold water. Add boiling water and salt and cook until thick. May need to stir often. Eat with milk and sugar.

Fried Corn Meal Mush

Cook mush recipe. Pour cooked mush into a bread loaf pan and let cool. Cut into half-inch slices and fry in a pan with oil. Eat with butter and syrup.

The recipes included in this book should not be tried without adult supervision.

Homemade Soap

5 POUNDS LARD OR 5 1/2 POUNDS CRACKLINGS
(CRACKLINGS ARE THE LEFTOVERS
AFTER RENDERING LARD.)
1 CAN LYE
1 1/2 GALLONS WATER

Stir occasionally the first day. Then set for three days. Cook until clear. Let set until hard and cut into bars.

The recipes included in this book should not be tried without adult supervision.

Stir Soap

1 CAN LYE
1 QUART WATER

Stir these together. Lye will cause heat so let cool.

ADD:
3 TABLESPOONS BORAX
1/4 CUP AMMONIA
1 PINT COLD WATER
4 PINTS MELTED GREASE
(LARD OR BEEF TALLOW)

Stir until it looks like honey. Pour into flat 12 x 16 inch pan or roasting pan so the mixture can be at least 2 inches thick. Let set one hour, and then cut. If it sets too long, it will crack when cut.

The recipes included in this book should not be tried without adult supervision.

I Double
Dog Dare You!

Dorie was sitting in the wagon with Jix and one of the barn cats.

"Now, you two do as I tell you," Dorie lectured the animals. "I am your teacher and today we are going to learn how to read." Dorie pretended the animals were students. Jix looked up faithfully at Dorie willing to do anything she commanded, but the calico barn cat looked as if she was ready to bail out of the wagon any second.

Dorie paused in her lesson as she saw Mick and Robbie walking toward her.

"What kind of trouble are you two headed for?" Dorie questioned her brothers. She wasn't sure how much longer she could keep Jix interested, and the cat had already jumped ship and headed to the barn to search for mice.

"We're headed to the river," Mick explained to Dorie. "Want to come with us?"

"You bet," Dorie could not get the words out of her mouth quick enough. "I am so hot I might melt," she added.

"C'mon then but no girl stuff today," Mick told her. "Us boys are looking for an adventure and a way to cool off."

"Okay," Dorie replied. She loved to be with her older brother. Although she would never admit it, there were times she was a bit scared by some of the things he would try. He was a risk taker for sure and Dorie knew it. Good thing Marley was busy in the house or she would give Dorie a lecture to end all lectures about hanging out with the boys and being a tomboy.

The three children headed toward the Elkhorn River that wended its way around the farm. At school Dorie heard Miss Hayes explain the Native Americans who lived in this part of the state called the area near the river Ta Ha Zouka. Miss Hayes went on to explain those words meant Horn of the Elk. The Native Americans chose these words because they thought the place where the river branched out looked like elk horns. Dorie guessed the name just stuck and that is why they called it the Elkhorn River today.

The heat radiated off the surface of the earth as the children trudged toward the water. They passed through the scorched and shriveled fields of crops that Stanley was feverishly trying to grow. As they neared the grove of trees that lined the river bank, Dorie saw some open field.

"Grab some of that grass over there," Mick called to Robbie and Dorie.

"For heaven's sake, what are you talking about, Mick?" Dorie called back a bit confused. She watched as both Robbie and Mick picked up a handful of mossy green grass and shoved it into their mouths.

"Mmmmmm, mmmmmm," Mick savored the grass in his mouth.

"Mick," Dorie reasoned, "Mother will kill you if she finds you eating grass. That can't be good for you!"

"Oh, Dorie, haven't you ever heard of sheep shower grass? This is not the kind of grass that grows in the yard. This is just like eating candy. Tastes just like a lemon drop only a little bit more tart, but it sure cools you off on a hot day like today. Just try some. I dare you." Mick shared his secret as he held out a handful to her.

Dorie was never one to back down from a challenge. She took the offered handful of grass, popped it into her mouth, and chewed. She hated to admit it but Mick was right. It did taste like a lemon candy drop and it refreshed her. She liked it!

Ready to move on to an adventure and, hopefully, a chance to cool off in the water, the three children pushed forward to the river bank. The drought had hit Nebraska hard. The previous few years of lack of rain and fierce heat had caused the water level of the river to drop. Mick pointed out to Robbie and Dorie the place on the bank where the river had been and then where the water level was now. When the children looked out into the river, they could see the tops of bushes and trees that had previously been covered by river water.

They removed their shoes and squished their toes in the sandy bank. Dorie reveled in the feel of the soil on her bare feet. As they walked along they dipped their toes in the water at the edge of the river. It felt so good! They came upon a section of the river where a tree had obviously fallen and deteriorated into sections. The logs spanned from one side to the other but there were gaps between them.

"There it is," Mick concluded. "There is our adventure today and our challenge. I dare you to hop from one log to the next and make it all the way to the other side without falling in the water. First one to reach the other side is the winner."

Dorie gasped, "Mick, Robbie is too little to try that, and you know mother would kill us if we fall in and come home soaking wet from river water."

"Oh, Dorie, I am not little!" Robbie corrected her. "And if you get a bit wet, well, like mother says, you aren't sugar and you won't melt."

Even Robbie is more of a risk taker than I am, Dorie thought. Well there was no way she was going to let that happen.

"All right then, boys," Dorie upped the ante. "I challenge you to a race. First one across the river has to do chores for the other two for an entire day. I double dog dare you!"

"You're on, Dorie," Mick boasted. "You know I am going to win that dare. Robbie, stay with me and you will be all right. Let's get ready to race."

Dorie, Robbie, and Mick took their places on the bank. Robbie started them, "Ready, set, go!"

They were off in a flash. Mick's long legs swung out first catching the edge of the first log before quickly leaping to the next. Robbie was fast and he took off next slipping in just before Dorie got started. Dorie was not far behind as she thrust her arms carefully out from her body to maintain her balance.

Mick was quick as a wink. He moved with athletic grace, skill, and speed and was quickly several logs ahead of Robbie and Dorie. His laughter and glee at being outside, free, and clearly in the lead could be heard loud and clear as Dorie and Robbie were silently trying to keep up with him.

Mick looked back over his shoulder to gloat at the other two. "Come on you two slow pokes," he taunted as he kept his forward progress going.

But what Mick had not accounted for was the beavers. It was obvious the log had been in this place in the river for quite some time. The beavers had done their work of chewing on the log and had created quite a hole. This log lay smack dab in the middle of the river and now was part of the course the children were racing on.

The log race.

Mick's feet kept moving as he looked back at his siblings. He did not notice the hole. Abruptly, one of his feet did not move but the other one kept going. His foot had slid into the beaver hole and was caught. Mick instantly flung his arms out to the side to regain his balance but it was too late.

With his foot caught, his body tipped one way and then the other. Finally he slid sideways, lost his balance, and crashed into the flowing water.

Dorie burst into laughter. Alarmed, Robbie called, "Mick, are you all right? Where are you?"

Mick's head bobbed up and he raised himself up from the fall. The water was low so there was no danger of drowning in that puddle. But Mick came up sputtering with anger and indignation.

"Gol darn it!" he moaned as he struggled to pull himself back up to the log and continue his race.

Dorie was upon him now and maybe by chance or maybe by choice her foot found his hand on the log. She stepped squarely onto Mick's hand as he yelped, "Ouch. Darn it, Dorie, watch out. That's my hand."

Dorie did not miss a beat but kept moving toward the opposite bank. Robbie stopped to see if Mick needed his help. Dorie kept moving as she heard splashing, struggling, and cursing from behind her.

"Winner!" Dorie gleefully called as she placed her feet triumphantly on the dry river bank on the other side. "You boys can share my chores. There are enough of them to keep both of you busy."

Minutes later a wet Mick followed Robbie over the last log and onto the bank where Dorie rested, her race firmly won.

"Not fair, Dorie, not fair," Mick whined. "My foot got stuck."

Dorie's only response was, "Too bad, Mick. That is just the way the cookie crumbles. Better luck next time."

Mick shook his head in disbelief at his loss. The three Archer children sat on the river bank, soaking their feet in the cool water. Dorie started to chuckle over the sight of Mick floundering in the river and soon she burst into unrestrained giggles. Her wicked giggles tickled Robbie's funny bone and he too began to laugh.

Mick gave them both a withering look, but he couldn't help himself either and soon all three children were rolling with laughter over the day's events along the Elkhorn River.

The lazy days of summer at the river.

Saturday Night in the City

THE NEARLY TRANSPARENT RAYS OF the tangerine sun filtered through the early evening sky. The Archer home was bathed in its hazy light. It was Saturday night and that was a special time for all of the Archers. However, each Archer had his or her own special reason.

Saturday night was bath night. The week's work of both farm and school was washed away in Anna's tin tub. Freshly washed clothes awaited the children, hair brushed and braided or adorned with a ribbon for the girls. For the boys hair parted and combed down into obedience. It was time to go to town.

Anna labored to prepare for the weekly trip. One of her contributions to the family was in the form of chickens. She kept as many as she could feed. The hens were as valuable as gold to her. The Archers used the eggs and meat as food for the family. But they also used the eggs as barter for items in the grocery store. They had little or no money to buy items like flour, sugar, and coffee so instead they traded eggs for these basic foods.

Anna clutched the edges of her apron and held them up to her body to create a makeshift bowl. Inside of this gathered apron bowl was chicken feed. She called out to the chickens in the farm yard.

"Come on now. Here chick, chick, chick. Come and get your dinner," Anna called needlessly as she spread the feed on the ground with her hands. It didn't take much convincing because the hungry chickens ran to gobble up the feed as fast as she could lay it down. The chickens managed to eat some insects from the yard along with the feed. Anna loved her hens, but when they stopped laying eggs she did not hesitate to grab them up and fry them for dinner for her family.

Lately, sometimes when Anna was working outside, a hobo would make his way up to the Archer house. Anna knew times were tough all over, and the hobos hopped the trains and stowed away inside of the boxcars looking for opportunity in a better place. They carried their bindle stiff with them containing all of the items they owned in the world.

Anna had a heart of gold and although the Archer family had little, she knew she had more than any hobo. She would give each hobo a small pancake and tell herself, "There, but for the grace of God, go I." The hobo would thank her and would sometimes give Anna a piece of tramp art. Her favorite hobo gift

Anna's prized chickens.

was a shelf made of twigs she kept on her wall. Sometimes they would give her a cigar box that had been decorated.

Anna's apron had many uses throughout her day. She wore it from morning until night. First and foremost it was to keep her dress clean. If she saw company coming up the road, she would quickly snatch the apron off and hang it up, smooth her clean dress, and she was ready for neighbors to visit. The apron also helped Anna do her work. She wiped off the table with the apron. If necessary she even used the ruffle at the bottom to wipe kids' runny noses. That apron was a vital part of her daily life.

Anna always had a towel slung over her shoulder. She kept it at the ready for any emergency that might come up. Sadly, Anna now used her towels as a shield from the dust. She would wet them and pack them around the window sills to try to keep out the invasion of dust. It never seemed to work, and some dust always found its way into the house but Anna kept trying. She would try to make light of the situation by saying, "The dust is red today, children. Oklahoma is blowing in over Nebraska."

Anna now placed the eggs she had gathered into a basket for safe keeping. She called out to Marley, "Go fetch up the butter from the well to take to town."

Anna's apron.

After Anna had churned the butter she would lower it into the cool well in a bucket. This would keep it fresh since they had no refrigerator or freezer.

She carefully packed the eggs and butter into a box. With these precious items Anna would barter and obtain the items her family needed but could not afford. Basic staples would be hers by trading eggs and butter for them. If they had enough to barter with, they might even be able to get shoes or overalls the growing children needed.

Stanley prepared for town by hitching Molly and Dan to the wagon. The family relied on these two horses as well as their own feet for their transportation. Molly and Dan were accustomed to the Saturday night ritual. They also knew there might be a small treat for their troubles.

Anna called, "Come, children, time to go."

As the children came down the stairs Marley held onto Maggie's small hand. Anna said a prayer as she gazed at Maggie, "Thanks be to God for healing Maggie and keeping her well." Anna thought back to those tough days of dust pneumonia and shuddered. She constantly watched the children for signs of illness. She knew the danger was not over yet. On those days when the dust blew in, Anna kept the children sealed inside the farm house to protect them.

The others bustled into the wagon in anticipation of the night to come and the family set off.

The family made their way to town in the wagon, passing others who were making the same journey, as they traveled down the rutted dirt road. They passed some on foot, some on horses,

Taylor's store on the main street of Oakdale.

while others rode in wagons as they did. Every once in a while they saw a vehicle. There were a few people, mostly business owners, in town, who were prosperous enough to afford one of the cars they sold up in Norfolk. Of course most were not new but it didn't matter because few could afford such a luxury, and the Archers marveled at the vehicles.

As the Archer family passed neighbors on the road, Stanley would greet them by raising his right hand up, still maintaining a grip on the reins. With his index finger he would give each one an almost invisible salute by turning his finger a quarter of an inch. Everyone responded in the same way. Then there were the vigorous waves from the children to fellow classmates and a few shouted out "hellos" as everyone in town converged on Taylor's grocery store.

The store was divided in half. One half contained the dry goods while the other held the groceries. Almost like magic the men went in one direction, some outside to play horseshoes, while the ladies headed in the other, each to do the important business of the night. The women ooohed and ahhhed over the new yard goods the Taylor store offered. If a family had extra money to purchase the yard goods, then a very lucky little girl would have a new dress soon. When the bartering had been done and the purchases of the night made, then the real business of the night began—fun!

Robbie questioned Dorie, "What movie do you think Mr. Taylor will show tonight?"

Dorie snickered, "Oh, Robbie, you know probably the same thing we always see. A shoot 'em up Western with cowboys and horses I am betting."

Taylor's outdoor movie theater.

Robbie replied, "I don't care. I love watching those cowboys and horses flash across that screen. I sure hope Mrs. Taylor makes popcorn for us." If they were particularly lucky, Mrs. Taylor would offer each child a free handful of popcorn, which was something salty to chew on and fill them up.

The children gathered out back of the store in anticipation of what awaited them. There on kegs of nails set long planks of wood. These simple benches were placed in front of a sheet suspended on a rope between two large oak trees. Later, when the darkness was complete the movie would be shown to the delight of the children.

If the god of fortune really smiled on them, and their parents had been able to sell all of their products, the children would be rewarded with a penny for some candy. What a choice they had then! What to buy? Should it be Boston Baked Beans or Chick O Sticks? Maybe Cherry Red Dots or Candy Buttons? Some would choose Chowards Scented Gum, but most children preferred whichever candy they could get the most of for their penny. It didn't happen often so the children relished and savored any candy they got.

The children were not the only ones to enjoy Saturday night. While their children were occupied with the movie, the adults had time to be together. After the business of the night had been concluded, the women and men of Oakdale gathered inside the store to catch up with each other, discuss the weather, and commiserate together over the dusters and grasshoppers.

Then the conversation would turn and the jokes would start. Each farmer tried to outdo the other with a funny story.

One farmer chided, "The birds had to fly backward out at my place to keep from getting sand in their eyes."

Another added, "My wife cleaned her pots and pans by hanging them up to the keyhole in the wall and letting the sand that blasted in through the hole do the scouring."

"That's nothing," the third farmer said, "Out at my farm it was so hot the hens laid hard-boiled eggs."

Laughter rang out over the store and for a few moments the difficulty of the dust bowl, the drought, and the ruined crops was forgotten.

On a particularly lucky night a rag-tag band of men would start to play music from the second floor of the store. After the movie and conversation everyone would head upstairs to listen to the band. Soon they were dancing.

The teenagers particularly liked this part of the night because they were able to ask that special someone they were sweet on to dance with them, under the ever watchful eye of parents, of course. Even the little ones danced and danced until they grew tired. Then an older sibling would carry them into the coat closet and gently lay them on a bench to slumber until it was time to go.

Together the families bartered, conversed, and danced until well after midnight when they gathered their sleepy children and headed home with their treasures.

It was late on that Saturday night. Marley had picked up a sleepy Maggie and deposited her in the coat room. Dorie watched as Mick danced with one pretty girl after another. She looked on as her parents twirled around the impromptu dance floor of the store. She saw something rare. She saw her parents smile.

Dorie looked around the room. Near the window was Marian with her parents. They were beaming with glee as they laughed over some shared joke. *Marian*, thought Dorie, *the girl who wore a feed sack shirt to school.* Next to Marian was Betty and her sister, Cheetie, the one who wore the flour sack underwear. Over in the far corner Dorie saw Sam. Tonight it didn't matter that his shoes were too big. He had taken his shoes off and was dancing up a storm in his bare feet.

It was at that moment Dorie realized a great truth. Times were hard for the Archers. They didn't always have enough to eat. Dust was everywhere. Grasshoppers invaded and ate everything. Clothes and shoes were worn and old.

But the truth was every family in the store was in the same boat. Everyone was going through hard times. No one had enough to eat. Dust and grasshoppers were in everyone's house and fields. Clothes were repaired and used and reused by every family. But on Saturday nights these families got together and got through tough times. They were able to weather the storm of the dusters and difficulties because they weathered it together.

That was it. Dorie grinned feeling very wise for her twelve years. That was the answer. There was no other way to survive but to count on and depend on each other. Dorie knew at that moment that she would be all right.

She knew, without a sliver of doubt, that her family would make it through until the rains began again, the dust stopped blowing in, and the grasshoppers disappeared. Together, community, friends, and neighbors held the answer to this dilemma. Together they were stronger than the dusters, grasshoppers, and drought, and together they would make it.

Dorie moved through the crowd of neighbors and friends toward her parents. Anna and Stanley were slowly dancing together to the beat of the music. Dorie tapped her father on the arm, looked up at his face, and said, "Excuse me, Sir and Madame, may I have this dance please?"

Stanley and Anna looked down at their daughter. They smiled and paused in their dancing. Stanley lifted Dorie up and placed her feet on top of his feet. Then Dorie put her hands over the intertwined hands of her parents. With the banjo playing, the three Archers danced on together through the dust-covered days of Nebraska, confident of brighter days ahead.

Dancing with destiny.

Eymann Family
Photo Album

Photo Analysis

1. List all of the items you see in the photo. Use words that are nouns.
2. Who is in the photo?
3. How are the people dressed?
4. What is the location of the photo?
5. When was the photo taken? Time of day? Season? Time of year?
6. What story does this photo tell?
7. Why did the photographer want to capture this image?
8. What caption would you write for this photo?
9. What is the most important thing about the photo?
10. What is surprising about this photo?
11. Why did this photo survive?
12. What do you think will happen next?
13. What questions does this photo create? Where could you find answers to your questions?
14. What else would you like to know about this photo?
15. How does this photo make you feel?
16. What prior knowledge can you connect with this photo?
17. Does this photo reflect anything about the way of life during this historical era? What do you know about this era?
18. Do you think this photo is an authentic historical record?

ELKHORN RIVER

Comprehension/ Discussion Questions

Prologue

1. How many years ago does the story take place?
2. Where does the story take place?
3. Describe a dust storm.
4. Who are the characters in the story?
5. Why is the date historically important? You may need to do some research!

Chapter One

1. Who are Molly and Dan and why are they vital to the Archer family?
2. How did Dorie and her siblings get to and from school?
3. What motto did Dorie's mother teach her? What does it mean? Do you think this is true?
4. What chores did the Archer children have to do?
5. Why were Dorie's parents worried?

Chapter Two

1. What present did Mick receive for Christmas? Where did it come from?
2. What is the setting for this chapter?
3. What unexpected thing happened to Dorie?
4. How did the Archer children help Dorie?
5. Expressions of the 1930s are different than our modern expressions. What do these expressions mean? How would you say this in modern day English? **Hold your horses. Holy mackerel! Gosh darn it!**

Chapter Three

1. What position did Mick Archer play in baseball?
2. How did the spectators keep cool?
3. What was the problem with the pitcher?
4. What unexpected thing did the batter do? Why?
5. Why was Mick the hero of the game?

Chapter Four

1. Describe a one room school house in your own words.
2. What did the family eat for breakfast?
3. What is the family going to do after school?
4. Describe the school day. How does the day change from morning to afternoon? What is the weather like? What can the children hear?
5. What do the Archer children do at the end of the chapter? How would you feel if you had to do the same thing as the Archer children? If this happened today what would the teacher and the children do differently?

Chapter Five

1. What were Mick and Stanley doing in the field?

2. What are the signs of drought in this chapter?

3. What is wrong with Maggie? What medicine do they give her?

4. Describe what happens in the field after lunch.

5. How do Stanley, Mick, and Dorie escape?

Chapter Six

1. Why did Anna ask Dorie to go to the river?

2. What is canning? Why did Anna can food?

3. Dorie hears a noise and makes a discovery. What does she find?

4. What is Dorie's bargain with her brother?

5. Expressions are important in this chapter also. What do these expressions mean and how would you say this in modern English? **Holy cow! The jig is up! Hold your horses.**

Chapter Seven

1. What preceded a dust storm?

2. What does this phrase mean? "…weather punctuated and defined the seasons."

3. Describe Dorie's feelings during the dust storm.

4. Describe the corn field after the dust storm passed.

5. Who does Dorie see in the field? What are they doing?

Chapter Eight

1. What is an outhouse? Why was an outhouse necessary?
2. Using your own words explain how to play the game of Runners.
3. Where did the children take a bath and how was it done?
4. Why did the Archer family need to go to town?
5. What problem did Dan have?

Chapter Nine

1. What is an Indian summer? Give a description using your own words.
2. What is wrong with Maggie in this chapter?
3. What homemade remedies do they use on Maggie?
4. What does Dorie do to soothe her sister?
5. What is Dorie's advice to Maggie?

Chapter Ten

1. How did Dorie stay warm in bed during the cold nights?
2. How is the Archer home heated?
3. What did Dorie see on the table? How was this used as communication in the 1930s?
4. What decision did Mick Archer make?
5. What do the letters WPA stand for and how was Stanley connected to the WPA?

Chapter Eleven

1. What is Mick doing as the chapter opens? Why is he doing this?
2. What is the weather like?
3. What surprise does Mick find in the road?
4. What was his secret wish?
5. What does Dorie say about the surprise gift?

Chapter Twelve

1. Why did Marley turn the dishes upside down?
2. What are the two ways to make corn meal mush? Which one would you like and why?
3. What is *remaking* a dress? Have you ever worn something that has been remade?
4. What is Dorie's problem?
5. Describe what happened to Dorie during the school day? What would you have done if you were in her place?

Chapter Thirteen

1. What does *double dog dare you* mean?
2. What kind of race did the children have?
3. What does *Ta Ha Zouka* mean and where does it come from?
4. What was the bet?
5. What happened to Mick?

Chapter Fourteen

1. Why was Saturday night special to the Archer family?

2. What is bartering? How did Anna barter?

3. What did the children do in town on Saturday night? The parents?

4. What was the last event of the night?

5. What did Dorie discover that Saturday night?

Acknowledgments

BARBARA EYMANN MOHRMAN: I would like to thank my aunts and uncles Mick, Doris, Chub, Bonnie, and Lucile, who are the real role models for the Archer family. Without your help and support this book could never have been written.

Thank you to my cousins who are a constant support system for me! Thanks to my family for their patience and most especially to my husband, Dave, for his unfailing support. A special thanks to Clare who loved Dorie from the beginning.

I owe a huge debt of gratitude to Wava who patiently listened to me tell Dorie's story and then created the amazing drawings in the book. Your talent is immense!

A sincere thanks to everyone at Concierge Marketing for helping bring Dorie to life.

WAVA J. BEST: I would like to thank my husband, Tom, and my family who have always supported me in my artistic endeavors. Tom is not only my greatest admirer, he is also my best critic.

Thanks to Barb for involving me in this wonderful adventure of *The Dust-Covered Days of Dorie Archer*. Her writing helped make my illustrations come alive.

A sincere thanks to the generation that grew up during this stressful and depressed time. Their perseverance shows that through faith, hard work, and solace in each other, anything was possible. This is the message I would like to pass on to the next generation.

About the Author

Barbara Eymann Mohrman is a lifelong educator who has taught Spanish and English as a Second Language. She attended Nebraska Wesleyan University where Nebraska Poet Laureate William Kloefkorn was her teacher. She received a master's degree in instruction and curriculum from the University of Nebraska at Kearney. She is the author of *Four Blue Stars in the Window: One Family's Story of the Great Depression, the Dust Bowl, and the Duty of a Generation* (www.FourBlueStarsintheWindow.com). This young adult novel is her second book.

About the Illustrator

Wava J. Best lives in her home state of Nebraska with her husband, Tom. They have three daughters and five grandsons. Wava started her love of art in her early years of elementary school and continues to develop her skills in two- and three-dimensional art. Although her main focus is in 3D, she has returned to her love of sketching and painting portraying *The Dust-Covered Days of Dorie Archer*. Illustrating this book has rekindled memories of growing up in northeast Nebraska.

Wava has received numerous awards in art at the local, state, and national levels. One of which was Women of Achievement in the Cultural Arts. Wava is a professional artist, well known in Nebraska for her 3D art. Her work was recently selected for a national show.

Made in the USA
Charleston, SC
21 October 2013